BELIEVING
IN HORSES
OUT WEST

BELIEVING
IN HORSES
OUT WEST

VALERIE ORMOND

VETERANS
PUBLISHING

Book cover and interior design by The Book Cover Whisperer:
OpenBookDesign.biz

Published by Veterans Publishing

 VETERANS
PUBLISHING

978-0-9851874-1-5 Paperback
978-0-9851874-3-9 ePub
978-0-9851874-2-2 Kindle
978-0-9851874-4-6 Adobe Digital Editions

FIRST EDITION

Dedicated to Jaime, horse rescuers, and ranchers

CONTENTS

CHAPTER 1

MONTANA

SADIE FAILED ONE OF the horses she rescued. She searched for the reason, and the answer became clear. Distracted with lessons, showing her horse, school, and volunteer work, she neglected helping find Sunny a home. Her other activities seemed unimportant now, but it was too late.

She stared at the map on her phone, calculating the distance to Montana. It might as well have been on the moon. Cowboys, big sky, and a rescue horse from Maryland. How had this happened?

She read the rescue's text again. "Hi, Sadie, great news — a ranch in Montana adopted Sunny! She left for her new forever home last week. I'll talk to your mom soon and fill her in on all the details. Thanks for saving her and making this possible. Take care!"

At the barn, she dumped her phone face down in her tack box to make the terrible news disappear. She had lost track of Sunny and had no idea what kind of home the mare went to. Worse yet, Montana bordered Canada, where they still slaughtered horses for meat. This was all her fault, and she was helpless to do anything about it.

Being with her own horse was the best chance she had of taking her mind off the situation. In Lucky's stall, she began her grooming routine. She ran the rubber curry comb over his hair, scrubbing circles on his body, bringing the dirt and dust to the surface.

A new, younger boarder at the barn peered over the stall gate. Hope wasn't much taller than the four-foot door. Watching Sadie work Lucky's tricolor coat, she asked, "Coming to ride?"

"Yes, and I'm hoping Lucky's in a better mood than I am."

"What's wrong?" She blinked.

"I'd rather not talk about it," Sadie answered, wishing she were young and innocent again, without the problems and pressures of being thirteen.

"Can I ride with you? It's more fun with other people, and it will make whatever's wrong better."

"Sure. We've never ridden together, but I love your pony." Hope's pony was a medium-sized buckskin of unspecified breeding, a full and fuzzy coat, and tons of personality. He reminded Sadie of a giant stuffed animal.

"Thanks! I'll meet you in the arena in a few minutes

then." Sadie had met Hope before but didn't know her yet. Hope's light brown ringlets framed her cherubic face graced with a perpetual smile.

Sadie continued to brush, her mood improving with every stroke. Lucky followed her every move with those giant brown eyes and turned his head to the right as she moved around to his right side. The two sets of eyes met, one human, one equine. Lucky hesitated, pulled back, and pawed the ground.

What did he sense in her? "Sorry, Lucky, it's not about you. Everything's fine with us. Let's have a good ride with a new friend."

Sadie finished tacking up and led her sixteen-hands high athletic horse into the arena. She hopped on and savored the simple rhythm of his walk while warming up his muscles. The warmth of his body radiated through her calves held to his sides. Her close contact English saddle came as close to riding without a saddle as could be, other than if she used a small jockey saddle. At five-foot-six already, she would never be a jockey, so no reason to ride like one.

She felt his long strides and the crisp spring air putting Lucky in a perky mood. She gave herself a lesson in her mind remembering all the things her instructors had taught her over the years. Heels down, shoulders back, eyes up, and breathe deep. She focused on each body part at a time, and Lucky responded by lengthening his steps even more. Yes, she was officially in a horse-crazy girl's horse heaven created by a simple sand riding ring and a responsive partner.

Hope arrived at the arena gate and announced, "Coming in." Sadie appreciated the excellent riding etiquette.

At the mounting block, Hope hopped on Robin in one smooth move as if she'd done this her whole life. She reached over, patted her pony's neck, and urged his stout body into a walk with a gentle squeeze of her legs.

"I like this arena because it's so open," Hope said, "but I want to ride on the trails someday. I'm not allowed to ride alone, especially outside."

Sadie said, "When my mom first said the same thing about the trails, it didn't make sense to me. But it turned out to be the right idea, and I got to meet more people here by riding on the trails with them. Hopefully, you'll find the same."

"Well, I'm glad you were here today because I got to ride!"

"Let's do it then. It's time for us to trot. Lucky's getting bored. What do you think?"

"I'll work on my sitting trot with Robin after a warm-up. He's bouncy."

"Practice makes perfect," Sadie said and urged Lucky into his non-bouncy trot. Sadie floated as the two became one in his even two-beat cadence. Her breaths matched his, and she could go on forever like this. He showed no signs of slowing down, channeling his energy into her. Eventually, her breath shortened, a clue for a break for both of them.

"What grade are you in?" Sadie asked to fill the silence and keep her mind occupied.

"I'm in fourth grade," Hope said, giving Robin a rest at the same time. "How about you?"

"I'm in seventh, but I should be in eighth. I went to school in Spain for a year. And while I wouldn't have traded that for anything, it got complicated when we came back to the States. It's okay, I like my class, even if I am the tallest one."

They continued walking their horses, Sadie making serpentine patterns back and forth across the arena to stretch out Lucky's neck and limbs.

"Spain! How exciting! I haven't been to any other countries. What was Spain like?"

"Different and fun. My dad's in the Navy, so we were stationed over there. I went to a school on base the first year we were there. Then I begged my parents to let me go to the school out in town to get to know the Spanish people and learn the language. I was a bit more adventurous back then."

"What was your favorite part of living there?"

Sadie thought about what seemed so long ago. "The Andalusian horses. I fell in love with Spain's Andalusian horses. They were one of the reasons I ended up getting this guy here, a half-Andalusian." Hope fell in step behind Sadie, letting Robin walk the same pattern.

Hope said, "Lucky's special. No one else looks like him, those colors, his full black mane and tail."

"Thanks, and Robin is special, too. Hey, I think we need to get back to work, don't you?" Sadie didn't wait for an answer and eased Lucky into a smooth canter, her favorite gait. His imaginary wings unfolded, and they flew around the ring with hooves barely touching the ground. She glided him through the center, changing directions, and ended with a gradual slowdown to a trot and then a walk.

She brought Lucky to a square halt and scratched his withers. He turned his head in the direction of the scratch, and she watched his nostrils rising and falling. Sadie understood the look in his eye to know the meaning: "Thanks, I needed that."

They cooled the horse and the pony down at a walk, and Sadie said, "I think you'll get to see we're all a barn family here. I hope you like it. And if you have any questions, I'm happy to help since I've been here for a while."

"Thanks, and it's nice to know another rider here."

Sadie and Hope had ridden for a full hour practicing

the sport they loved aboard the partners in the sport they loved more. Back at Lucky's stall while taking off his tack, Sadie was relieved to have not been the only one there today. Sometimes she enjoyed the solace of the barn; this had not been one of those days. She didn't want to talk about Sunny but didn't want to be alone either.

Lucky nuzzled Sadie's shoulder for attention. Tension released from her body with the nudge, and she patted his neck under his mane where he liked it.

"Thanks, buddy," she said, knowing it was time to go.

Sadie traveled the one hundred yards from Loftmar Stables back to her house catching the scent of fresh-cut grass and the pastures. Non-horse lovers complained about the smell of manure, but horse lovers found the aroma a gentle reminder of the animals bringing them joy.

Lucky knew something was wrong and tried to make Sadie feel better. She sensed it, and that alone made her feel better for the moment. Something would happen to help her make this Montana situation right.

A perfect Lucky and a sweet Hope; this had to be one of those "signs" Grandma Collins spoke about. Lucky and Hope — a coincidence or a sign? Sadie took it as a sign.

CHAPTER 2

NO ONE UNDERSTANDS

"THERE YOU ARE," MOM said, as soon as Sadie opened the door. "Did you get my text?"

"Mom, I don't text and ride, you know." She regretted how snotty it sounded the minute it came out.

From the next room, Dad said, over his reading glasses, "There's no reason to snipe at your mother. That's not like you. What's wrong?"

"Nothing!" She stormed upstairs.

So much for the moment of feeling better. She looked in the mirror and didn't like who she saw. Dad was right. The barn's magic wore off too fast. She washed her hands and retreated to her room, pulling her cell phone out of her riding pants. They were the special breeches her mom bought her with a cell phone pocket on them, so she wouldn't lose her phone in case she got separated from her horse. It had happened before, and her mom had come to the rescue.

She read the text: "Come home as soon as you can cuz Dad's taking us out to a Friday night dinner for your favorite — Chinese!"

Sadie peeked out the crack of her door and hollered down the stairs, "Got the text, Mom. Sorry, I'll be right down." Over the lump in her throat, she croaked, "Thank you."

Her brother Austin popped out of his room and said, "Better hurry, they close at ten." He tapped his watch like Dad did.

Sadie smiled. Austin knew something was wrong without even knowing what it was. That's what years of having Sadie as a little sister instilled in him. She shut her door, changed out of her barn clothes, and brushed the helmet head look out of her thick, straight hair. She touched the lock of Lucky's tail hairs hanging off the corner of her dresser mirror and chanted to herself, "I believe; I believe; I believe." Her mantra had worked in the past, and she didn't know what else to do.

Dad was unusually chipper while they loaded up in the family SUV. Chinese was Dad's favorite, but it couldn't be the food. Could he be trying to make up for her being so cranky?

He broke her train of thought asking, "How was your ride?"

"Lucky was excellent, and I got to ride with one of the new boarders. It was fun."

"So what's the problem then?" His eyes met hers in the rearview mirror, and she couldn't avoid the conversation.

"Nothing too bad, only that I failed at one of the most important things I ever had to do."

"Oh, come on, Sadie," Mom said. "Don't be so hard on yourself."

Dad asked, "Can someone clue me in?"

"Me, too," Austin chimed in, looking up from his phone.

Mom started, "We found out today —"

"It's okay, Mom. I'll tell them. It was my mistake."

Mom nodded.

"Mrs. Heritage from Freedom Hill sent us a text today telling us one of the rescue horses is on her way to Montana!"

Sadie responded to Dad's curious expression in the mirror. "I was supposed to follow up on my horses to make sure they stayed in the right hands! Nobody seems to understand how bad this is."

"You need to add me to that list of people who don't understand," Dad said. "I'm not following this. The rescue found a home for a horse. Isn't that what you wanted?"

"Yes, Dad, but how am I going to check on Sunny in Montana?"

"I'll bet she went to nice people who will understand your interest in her well-being. You can email them, text, video chat, whatever, lots of ways to stay in touch. If we could do it from here to Afghanistan, Montana should be nothing."

"It's not the same." He didn't understand. Sadie viewed this as a colossal failure on her part. She knew more than he did about horses going to bad homes, not to mention the one hundred thousand horses a year going to slaughter. The pictures and videos she'd seen, and many times horse owners had no idea about their horse's fate. She shuddered thinking of the scenes back at the horse auction where she first found Sunny.

"Earth to Sadie," Dad brought her back.

Sadie fought back tears and faked a smile to her dad.

Mom interjected, "Go ahead and tell Dad about Sunny's new home."

Sadie sat up straight and exhaled. "Sunny is going to a ranch in Montana. Mom spoke to Mrs. Heritage who said it's one of those dude ranches where people go who pretend to be cowboys, well, and cowgirls, I guess. Montana! It couldn't be much farther away and still be in this country!"

"Sounds like a fantastic home. Wouldn't most horses

want to live out there like home on the range? Why is this such a bad thing?" Dad asked, as he continued driving.

"Because I'll never see her again! And I didn't even get to say goodbye to her because she's already gone. Don't you understand? I failed her. I have no idea what kind of home she's in." The passengers remained quiet.

"Well then … let's go see her," Dad said in his matter-of-fact way.

"What? We can't go see her. She's going to be two thousand miles away. I already looked it up."

"But you said she's going to a dude ranch. Let's go. Why not? I have tons of leave time I need to use. We're a military family; we're up for an adventure." Dad turned to Mom, his smile beaming.

Sadie's wheels turned in her head, and her spirits lifted like a bird taking flight.

"That's a wonderful idea. I wish I had thought of it," Mom said, and bumped Dad's elbow with hers on the armrest.

Reality set in, and Sadie said, "But, Dad, you and Austin don't ride. Why would you go to a dude ranch?"

"For you, kiddo. And it's not like I've never ridden a horse. Remember, I grew up in Texas. It'll be like riding a bicycle; I'll get back on."

"And you, brother?" Sadie pushed.

"Come on, I've watched you in enough lessons and

shows to have picked up a thing or two. I can take a lesson back at the barn before we head out. Don't worry about me. I like adventures."

Sadie sat back, then said, "I guess it's settled then. We're going to Montana. Thank you, Dad! And Mom. This will be epic!"

"Yeeha," Dad kidded, pretending to tip his fake cowboy hat.

CHAPTER 3

THE GOLDEN PAVILION

SADIE AND HER FATHER made a habit out of finding their favorite Chinese restaurant every time they moved. Maryland was the sixth place she had lived during her father's Navy career, and she and Dad had followed this ritual each time for as long as she could remember. As soon as he returned from Afghanistan, they searched for their new favorite in Bowie. Their third try took them to the Golden Pavilion, the hands-down winner, and the search was over.

The elderly gentleman in a tuxedo-style suit seated the Navarros in a corner booth and distributed the tall red menus with gold-embossed English and Chinese writing on the cover. He said, "Thank you for choosing to dine with us, and enjoy your meal." Dad talked to everyone, so Sadie knew from a previous visit that the gentleman who sat them was Mr. Lee, the proud owner of the family business established in the 1960s.

Sadie asked, "Do you want me to start trying to make reservations at the ranch? The name is Homeplace, by the way. I like that."

"Right now?" Mom asked.

"Why not?"

"Because we're here for dinner, for one. Also, we need to figure out when's the right time. Dad and I work, and you're in school. I know you're anxious, but we have some planning to do. We only decided to go on the way here."

"Tell you what," Dad said. "Let's get our orders in, and then Sadie can look up the ranch and tell us more about it. We can all learn more. Deal?"

"Sure, Dad." Sadie studied her menu. She listened to her brother and parents discuss menu items, and it was obvious the family did not share her enthusiasm for the trip. Were they going to talk about every item on the ten-page menu?

The waitress showed up, introduced herself with a bright smile, and asked, "Can I answer any questions about the menu, or are you ready to order?"

"Is everybody ready?" Dad asked. Fortunately, everyone nodded.

Sadie waited until the server walked away until she

pulled out her phone. She didn't want to seem ungrateful for this dinner treat, but she couldn't keep her mind off the idea of going to a ranch in Montana to check on Sunny.

What had seemed like an insurmountable problem earlier had been solved with one decision and one sentence out of her dad's mouth.

While working on her search for Homeplace Ranch, Sadie heard her mom talking about work in the background. Trying not to be rude, she looked up and listened for a minute. Mom worked for the Office of Naval Intelligence, which Sadie found exciting. Her mom did, too. Sadie was proud of both of her parents for serving their country in their own ways.

Mom stopped mid-sentence and said, "Sadie, I thought you were going to tell us more about the ranch? Get to work, girl!"

She could tell Mom felt bad about shutting her down earlier. If anyone in this group had an understanding of how bad Sadie felt about losing track of Sunny, it was Mom.

"Since you asked, here you go." Sadie viewed the images and words on her phone deciding which to talk about first. "Homeplace is in Utica, Montana, and the pictures are gorgeous! It's a family ranch, and the main reason people go is for the ranch experience, like riding.

There are a lot of other things to do there, too, like fishing, hiking, biking, archery, and events at night."

"You sound like a commercial," Austin said.

"There's a ton of information here, and I could go on and on. You will need to see it for yourselves when the time is right."

"We can do that," Austin said. "Sounds fun so far."

"Since we're still waiting for dinner, let's talk about timing, Liz," Dad said to Mom.

"It says here they are open for guests between May and September, so that's a start," Sadie said.

"You two will be out of school in June," Mom said. "I should be able to take a week off then. How about you, Dad?"

"That should work well since it's the beginning of the summer vacation time. Let's pick a week and see if they can take us." Dad seemed happy about the trip.

Austin pulled up the calendar on his phone. "We get out of school on June fifteenth; it's already on my calendar. So any time after that should work."

Dad said, "I'll call Homeplace and talk to someone about a week in June, then."

Sadie hid her disappointment. June was two months away. She looked around at the restaurant's ornate oriental furnishings and focused on the colorful fish swimming in the oversized fish tank decorated with bright pavilion statues, bridges, gates, and rocks. They reminded her of how she was going to be swimming around aimlessly for the next few months waiting for the time to pass.

"Spring rolls and soup are here," the tiny waitress said, placing the orders on the table.

"Maybe they will let me ride Sunny when we're there," Sadie said, after a bite of a tasty spring roll dipped in duck sauce.

"They should. You saved her, and you're a wonderful rider," Mom said.

She hadn't ridden Sunny. A local horseman generously donated his time to help train her while she lived at Freedom Hill. He helped a number of their rescues over the years. Homeplace must have seen something in her to want to adopt her into a program where not all people who vacationed rode regularly. She was ecstatic with the thought of reuniting with the mare she had purchased from the Hamilton Auction for $650, even if the reunion wasn't going to be for two months.

"Grandma Collins!" Sadie said. "We need to let her know. This all happened so fast, I forgot her Over-70 Surf Club sponsored Sunny at Freedom Hill for her first six months."

"You're right," Austin said. "I'll bet she'll want to go. Let's tell her tomorrow. It looks like there's enough food coming to feed a few families."

The flavors filled the air — fresh vegetables, onions, curry, Chinese spices, and sweet and sour made Sadie's mouth water. She stopped dominating the conversation to enjoy the family meal at her favorite place. They ate as much as they could and boxed up the rest in the traditional Chinese restaurant white cardboard trapezoid boxes with metal handles.

"Okay, it's fortune cookie time. I'll go first," Dad said. He always went first; it was part of the regimen. "*Every flower blooms in its own sweet time.*"

"That was a dumb one. Bad day for the fortune cookie maker," Austin said.

"Hey, it's springtime, isn't it?" Dad defended his fortune.

"I'll go next," Mom said, following the usual order. "*Keep your face to the sunshine, and you will never see shadows.*" She nodded, appearing content with her fortune. "Austin?"

"*Good news will be brought to you by mail.*" Austin tossed his fortune in the air over the table. "I think I had the same fortuneteller as Dad."

Sadie read hers, trying to figure it out. "*If a true sense of value is to be yours, it must come through service.*" She tucked it into her pocket to think about what it meant. To her, no one else at this table understood her feeling of total failure.

CHAPTER 4

THE

HORSEKEEPER

THE NEXT MORNING, SADIE couldn't wait to tell someone about the trip. "Mom, I'm going next-door to see Brady! And then I'm headed to the barn for a few minutes if that's okay."

"When have you ever gone to the barn for a few minutes? Give our best to Brady, please."

Brady moved in next-door last year, and Sadie took him under her wing and made sure the horse-loving bug bit him. She counted the seventy-five steps from her family's farmette to Brady's grandfather's rancher. She reached through the torn screen and knocked on the door.

"Hi, Sadie!" the eleven-year-old blond boy answered.

"Guess what?"

"What?" He smiled.

"That's not what I mean. This isn't a knock-knock joke. Guess where I'm going?"

"To the moon? To the barn? Can you give me a hint?"

"Well, it has to do with horses, so the barn was close."

"To another horse show? To the Olympics?"

"Now you are way off. I guess I need to tell you. We're going to a dude ranch! Out West, in Montana!"

"We are?" His face lit up like she had never seen, and she watched his eyes dancing with imagination.

Sadie had chosen the wrong words. She hated when she did that! She thought fast.

"Well, I came here to ask you a favor."

"You know I'd do anything for you. Name it."

"I need you to keep an eye on Lucky while I'm gone." His smile disappeared, and he looked down. She read that to mean he understood the "we" she mentioned did not include him.

Within seconds, he looked back up, head cocked, and asked, "You would trust me?"

"Yes, or I wouldn't ask! Remember, you are Lucky's 'groom,' and he loves you and trusts you. I wouldn't think of asking anyone else unless you want me to."

"No, no, no way. My first time being an almost-horse-owner, and I'm not going to let you take that away from me."

Sadie respected how well this kid took disappointment

and turned it around to something positive. "Let's make it sound more official than an almost-horse-owner, how about a foster owner?"

She saw his face collapse again. Oh, no! What had she said this time? "Brady Battles, what's wrong?"

"You haven't called me that in a long time." He said, quiet now.

"Well, I haven't seen you look like this since that terrible incident at school."

"Yeah, and you had to save me. I'll never forget that. You were my first real friend. Anywhere."

"If I'm still your friend, then tell me what's wrong. All I said was…"

"I heard what you said." He paused. "When my dad gets mad at me, which he does a lot, he tells me if I keep acting up, I'll end up in a foster home. That's all."

That's all! It was Sadie's turn to not let Brady see her emotions. She wasn't sure if she was more angry or sad. Who could say that to a child? Especially this child! She focused on the front porch deck's peeling paint, searching for words.

"I'm sorry for the poor choice of words on my part. I think anyone would be lucky to have you as a part of their family. How about if we call you Lucky's horsekeeper? Like a zookeeper, or a beekeeper? Will that work?"

"Sure. That's a lot less lame than almost-horse-owner,

right? The horsekeeper has a certain ring to it. I'll even think about starting a horsekeeping business and taking care of other people's horses when they are on vacation. What do you think?"

Now he was back. "Not until you are finished with Lucky, you don't! This isn't going to be easy, but you are up to it. Let's go back to the barn and talk about what you'll do."

"I'm up for it! I can go like this. My sneakers will do, even if they aren't the best for the job."

They climbed the hill between their houses and the barn. Sadie said, "With all the money you make as a horsekeeper, you can buy yourself a set of boots."

"Yeah, and we can make a flier and hang it at the barn to tell people about my business. And then I can buy other stuff, too!"

"Great idea! One day you will be on the TV show, *Shark Tank*, and one of the millionaires will want to partner with you and your horsekeeping business!"

"Why not?" he shrugged. "But, Sadie, you came over to tell me about your trip, and all we've done is talk about me. I want to hear about it ... even if it is without me since you need me here to watch Lucky. I understand."

This kid. "Oh, it's no big deal. I need to go out West to check on one of the horses I rescued. And my dad thought it would be fun if we all did it as a family trip.

My Grandma Collins is coming, too, because she's not one to miss an adventure!"

"I hope you'll take lots of pictures, and I'll send you pictures of Lucky every day. Speaking of him, here we are. Let's go find out what he's up to and let him know there's going to be a new sheriff in town." Brady faked a swagger walk like he was a cowboy entering a saloon.

Sadie shook her head and laughed at her special, silly friend, who was so many layers deep and the kindest soul she had ever known.

CHAPTER 5

WHO AM I?

ONCE THE EXCITEMENT WORE off, Sadie had doubts about the trip. Who was she to determine if a horse was being well taken care of? What did she know about ranch horses? Was she going to tell some man who had been running his family ranch for decades how to treat his horses? And worse, what could she do if Sunny was being mistreated? People who mistreated animals were mean, as she'd seen in the past. Was she putting her entire family at risk?

She'd had time to think since time had passed. Perhaps her initial reaction was an overreaction?

Perhaps she gave herself too much credit in being the only one who could save Sunny. After all, Freedom Hill wouldn't let her go to a bad home; they had rules and regulations for adopters, screened homes, and found horses new homes for a living. All Sadie had done was save ten horses once, and she'd already lost track of one in Montana.

Her phone rang, and she saw the word "Grandma" pop up on the screen. Grandma cheered her up and always had answers for everything. Sadie picked up and said, "Hi, Grandma. I'm glad you called."

"Are you okay?"

"Sort of."

"You don't sound okay," Grandma said. "You can tell me."

"I've been thinking about the trip."

"Me, too! I can't wait. Time can't pass fast enough. You should see my new outfits — consignment shops, of course — the best bargains. I even took some Western riding lessons to brush up. You know I used to ride a long time ago. I think that's where you get it. But it's been back in the saddle like I never left except for newfound creaks and pains." She laughed.

Sadie blurted out, "I'm having doubts."

"Doubts about what? Live life to your fullest; you're only young once. Are you worried about letting me come along? Oh, honey, I promise I won't get in any trouble in Montana. And I won't embarrass you by telling everyone how famous you are."

"Thank you, Grandma, I appreciate that, especially since I'm not famous. I guess my thinking is, who am

I to decide if Sunny's in the right hands? And if she's not, what would I do? I'm thirteen, and I don't know everything about horses."

"Who does? And you'll be fourteen by then, sweetheart, another whole year smarter than thirteen. You don't need to know everything. Rely on your instincts because you have the best. Well, besides me, that is."

"But still —"

"Here's an idea, why don't you call Freedom Hill? Ask them what to look for, like a checklist. They must have something like that. Ask them what to do if something doesn't seem right. I'm sure they're not going to tell you to handle it on the spot by yourself," Grandma said.

"Why didn't I think of that? At least I'll feel prepared, like having a clue about what I am doing. I knew you'd know what to do."

"We're a team, remember? If you hadn't trusted me enough to tell me, I couldn't have helped. That's what I'm here for."

"Thanks, Grandma, I'll call right now."

"And remember — you have to believe you can do it. Bye … and love you." She hung up.

Grandma made it sound so simple. Arm herself with knowledge from the horse rescue, follow her instincts, and believe she could do it. Sadie scrolled through her contacts and came to Mrs. Heritage. She would understand. The phone rang and rang, so Sadie left a voicemail message.

She watched the clock and thought about what she would say. Maybe it was a good thing Mrs. Heritage didn't answer. She jotted down notes to help. Picking up the book she was reading for school, she read enough pages of *Where the Lilies Bloom* to keep her on track and able to pass the next quiz. She wanted to hit the barn.

Lucky grazed in the pasture along with the other geldings and raised his head as she walked by. Sadie held out a carrot while standing by the gate, and the bribe worked. She attached his halter and lead rope and led him to his stall where he pulled at his hay net.

"You can't be hungry; you were eating outside." He turned to her lazily and went back to his hay. Sadie groomed him trying to help shed out his winter coat. "We're not going to ride today, handsome boy, I only wanted to see you. I think you'd rather be eating anyway." She laughed at herself. Interesting how being in a horse's presence can change a mood.

The phone rang, and Sadie realized she'd forgotten about her dilemma with the trip. Leaving Lucky's stall, she answered, "Hi, Mrs. Heritage, thanks so much for calling back."

"Hello to you, young lady. How are you?" The accomplished horse saver's melodic voice calmed her.

"I'm fine, thank you, but I wondered if you could help me with something for Sunny."

"Well, you are the one helping us by going all the way out to Montana to check on her, so what do you need?"

"I might be better prepared if I have ideas of what to look for when I get there. I mean, I would know obvious things like if she's skinny or if she looked anything like she did at the auction. But I figured you guys are the experts at knowing what to do."

"As a matter of fact, many of the rescues in Maryland work together, and we do keep a list of issues to observe. We use it when we go on site to assess situations. I can send it to you if you're interested. Thanks for asking!"

"My Grandma came up with the idea, but I agreed."

"I can't tell you how happy we all are that you are going to check on her. We talked with the ranch owner many times, and he seems like such a nice man. Tell Mac we said 'hi' when you get there, won't you?"

"Okay and thank you. I'll say hi from the whole Freedom Hill gang. Sorry to take so much of your time, so I'll be going. Bye-bye." That sounded so childish.

"Don't worry about my time, and please call back with any more questions. If I don't hear from you again, have a wonderful trip. I'm jealous!"

Sadie felt better with something official to use to help judge the state of the horse. She pulled Lucky's face out of the hay, put on his halter, and led him back up the hill. When she got to the gate, Thor stood there. Thor was one of the horses she rescued who turned out to be a real champion. Sadie opened the gate, removed Lucky's halter, and he cantered down the hill to join his horse buddies.

Thor stayed by her side. She scratched his neck, and he stared straight at her. Memories flooded her brain with stories of horses in bad homes, and an image of the hundreds of sad horses at the auction bombarded her. Despite her doubts, she had to go check on Sunny. Thor reinforced that decision.

CHAPTER 6

HOMEPLACE RANCH

On Sunday, June twentieth, Sadie, and her family arrived at Homeplace Ranch after a scenic ride through Big Sky Montana in one of the ranch's shuttle vans. The final miles stretched down a bumpy dirt road without a house or building in sight. Fields of lush green grass poured into hills meeting the bluest of blue skies dotted with fluffy white clouds. God must have painted it that way.

Grandma Collins had arrived at the airport from California wearing a stylish cowboy hat, already looking the part of a cowgirl. She said, "I'm sorry you all had to wait for me so long; you should have gone ahead without me."

"It was nothing, Mom," Sadie's mother said. "We didn't want to ask poor Cody here to make a separate trip for you. Besides, this way we experience it all together."

Cody, the driver, took the final turn into the property where they entered under the wooden arch reading Homeplace Ranch. A long log cabin appeared on the right with tall windows on the front and the back so people could see the country landscape right through the building. Wood hitching posts decorated the front, and a series of benches and tables provided comfortable gathering places for guests. Absorbing it, Sadie thanked Sunny for leading them to Montana.

The van stopped, and Cody turned to everyone with a genuine smile and said, "Welcome to Homeplace." He seemed glad to be back. He opened the doors and said, "You can leave your bags in here, and I'll drop them off at your cabins while Mac greets you. C'mon into the main lodge, and we'll get you settled in."

Austin said, "I can help if you want, because my grandmother brought enough bags to stay a month, not a week." He and Sadie laughed, and Mom looked embarrassed.

"You leave her alone, kids. She's trying to be prepared. She'll get the last laugh when you all need something she packed because she thought about it and you didn't," Mom said, sticking up for her mom.

Sadie tried not to gawk like a tourist, but there was so much to see in the lodge. Cowboy art on the walls, furniture made from animal horns, bronze sculptures of horses bucking, and cow and deer hides were strewn about in the right places. This was more like a museum than what Sadie had in mind when she thought of a ranch. She loved it, and she hadn't even been here five minutes.

A white-haired gentleman with sun-kissed skin and a smile as broad as his cowboy hat brim came forward to greet them. "Welcome to our home, which is your home until you leave. I'm Mac, and this here is my lovely wife, Keela."

"It's a pleasure to meet you," Keela said holding a tray full of glasses. "I thought you might be parched after the long trip. Here's some sweet tea."

"Best in the state, too," Mac said, winking.

"That's thoughtful of you, ma'am," Austin said and reached for one of the chimney glasses topped with a fresh cut lemon slice. He took a swig, licked his lips, and declared, "Yep, has to be the best in the state."

"Let me introduce everyone," Dad said. "I believe you've already met my joker of a son, Austin." He put his hand on Austin's shoulder. "This is my wife, Liz. I'm Jim, and this is our daughter, Sadie. And this is my mother-in-law, Anna Collins."

Mac said, "We've had the pleasure of getting to know Mrs. Collins over the phone. She told us about her surf club and how they sponsored Sunny. She also told us about you, Sadie, the famous horse saver."

"Of course I did! Not everyone can do what she did. I'm proud of my girl. And look at her here today, across the country to check on one of her horses."

Sadie turned pink and glanced around to see if anyone was within earshot, happy to find an empty room. So much for Grandma's promise not to brag on her.

Mom saved her. "I'll take one of those teas, please, Keela. It's been a long day getting here."

Sadie said, "Me, too," and reached for one. "What a nice place, Mr. MacKenney, and not what I expected at all. I pictured sawdust floors."

"We have that, too, for the horses. A lot of the younger folks call me Mr. Mac, for short. For now, I wanted to welcome you. Keela will explain where you'll be staying and give you your cabin keys and maps of the property. You'll find hospitality packets in your cabins with descriptions of our activities to help get you acquainted. We'll all be meeting up at six o'clock for supper in the dining hall, and you'll meet more of our crew and mingle with the other guests."

"Mac will lay out the plan for the week and discuss options available like fishing, hiking, biking, and more," Keela said. "So come on in the office with me, and I'll get you on your way so you can rest up and build up an appetite before the evening meal."

Sadie squinted at an old photograph directly across

from her. She recognized a face, sort of. A radiant blonde wearing a white and gold glitter sash sat astride a muscled bay horse who had to be a barrel racer. The young woman's smile matched the brightness of the sash, radiating pride. It was Keela, the former Rodeo Queen.

The Navarro group made their way to their cabins passing other ones on the way. Sadie followed the map, although she could have followed the color-coded signs lining the route pointing in the directions of the destinations. Each cabin had a name, and their cabin was Kalispell, a Montana city which meant flat land above the lake.

The log cabin smelled of pine and had high ceilings, hardwood floors, and rustic wood furnishings. Brightly colored quilts covered the beds, and Western-themed paintings adorned the walls. The living area included overstuffed chairs, a gas fireplace, and an out-of-place flat screen TV. The luggage sat neatly stacked in the room.

Sadie darted from room to room. A brook ran right outside their window.

Mom said, "I'm going to put my feet up and relax. Dad, do you want to join me?"

"Sounds like a plan. We've been on the move since early this morning. Okay, guys, stay out of trouble, while I can't imagine there's much trouble to get into out here." He shrugged and followed Mom into their bedroom.

"Be ready to go before six," Mom called over her shoulder. "We don't want to be late to the first event."

Sadie and Austin eyed each other and said in unison, "Yes, Mom."

Sadie said, "This is so unbelievable; I don't know what to do next. I don't want to put my feet up."

"I'm going to text Katie and let her know we made it. I'll try not to make it sound as good as it is, so she doesn't feel bad about not being here," Austin said, talking about his girlfriend.

Sadie didn't have a boyfriend to text. "I'll call Brady and check on Lucky."

"If you do, he might think you don't trust him. It hasn't even been a day yet. Remember, he's doing you a favor. Don't abuse it."

"Okay, I'll wait until tomorrow."

"If you're so antsy, why don't you go see Grandma? She's probably dying to show someone her new digs. Check the map and follow the signs. You'll find it."

"I'll do that. Good idea — be back soon." Sadie headed out the door on her way to the Helena cabin. She took in every sight and sign of wildlife. She watched a bird, probably a hawk, circling above and stopped in her tracks. After all, she wasn't in a rush. The two months of waiting was over; she was finally here.

Sadie loved what had easily become her new home

for the week and wondered how she had ever hesitated to come here.

～

CHAPTER 7

SUNNY

WITH TIME ON HER hands, Sadie took a detour on the way to Grandma's to get a closer look at the horses she'd seen in a corral on their way to their cabin. Her family was more interested in getting to the cabin than checking out the horses, so she didn't stop and slow them down. She was on her own and free to do what she wanted, an exhilarating feeling.

She retraced her footsteps to the lodge and came across the corral with the scenic and practical five-rail post-and-rail wooden fence. Everything seemed natural here like it grew out of the ground.

Horses stood around in the corral, and cowboys and two cowgirls untacked a handful of horses tied to hitching posts outside. She kept her distance to stay out of their way. They worked with precision unhooking the big Western saddles and removing their headstalls, replacing them with halters and lead ropes before tying them to the posts.

Sadie recalled her list from Freedom Hill. These horses were well-fed, and their coats glistened. They swished their tails and stomped at flies like every other horse. There weren't any ears pinned or other signs of annoyance. She scanned the herd looking for a palomino mare and didn't find one among the approximately twenty horses of every size, breed, and color. The group included chestnuts, or sorrels as they call them out West, grays, Pintos, bays, spotted, and a coal-black one.

She went to the far side of the corral away from the people unsaddling the horses and leaned on the fence to get a better view. A young cowboy in brown leather chaps with fringes wearing a black cowboy hat approached her. Was she not supposed to be here? But he didn't look like he was going to say something like that. Instead, he smiled and greeted her. "New here?"

He looked familiar, but she didn't know anyone here. At least she didn't think she did. Good looking, she surmised he knew it. Oh, right, he asked her a question.

"Yes, we got here about an hour ago."

"Didn't take long for you to find the horses, did it?" That smile again with whiter-than-white teeth, and something about those blue eyes. "Name's Blake, welcome."

He reached out to shake her hand, which seemed odd for someone his age.

He worked here, so he probably had to be nice to guests. "Thank you, and I'm Sadie." She shook his warm, strong hand.

"Are you looking for someone? Picking out your ride for tomorrow?"

Would he ever stop smiling? "No, well, sort of. I hoped to see Sunny, the palomino Quarter Horse."

"Kind of particular, aren't we, for having been here an hour?" Sadie couldn't tell if he was kidding or not. She figured he was at that age where guys like him enjoy picking on younger girls. A foot taller than her, he could probably lift a bale of hay in each hand.

"I guess so. I didn't mean because I was picking her out to ride; I didn't think it worked that way at these places. I wanted to see her because she's the whole reason I'm here."

"Oh, I got it. I know who you are now. You're the kid who rescued the horse, and you're out here to make sure we know what we're doing. Cute." He smirked at her.

Blood rushed to Sadie's face, and she tried to force her temper back down before she said something she didn't want to say. But that didn't work. "I'm glad you think it's cute. You didn't see her at the auction where I had to keep the meat buyers from getting her. Have you ever been to one of those auctions?"

"Easy there, I didn't know it was such an issue. Sorry about that. Do you want to see her or not? I know where she is, and you won't find her here." The smile finally disappeared.

She didn't want to go anywhere with this guy but nodded yes.

"She's over here in the barn along with some others." She followed him to a two-story red barn with white trim and the ranch's brand symbol over the large double doors. The brand was a circle with a horizontal line beneath it. Despite being curious about its meaning, Sadie was not about to ask this jerk. In reality, she didn't want to say anything and already regretted not going directly to Grandma's cabin.

Blake spoke up; Sadie guessed because he had to be a tour guide for people like her. "She's on stall rest. We put them on stall rest when they may be injured or —"

"I know what stall rest is," Sadie interrupted.

"Hey, I'm sorry we got off to a bad start. Can you let it go? Like it or not, I'm going to be here all week, and you'll be seeing a lot of me."

She didn't like it. Why did he treat her like a child? Was she being childish? Think like an adult. "Why is she in?"

"She came up lame yesterday, nothing serious, and our vet checked her out. She'll be fine, but we wanted to give her an extra day of rest as a precaution." He stopped at the third stall in. "Here she is." He reached in his pocket, pulled out a treat, and gently fed it to her over the stall door. "She's a pretty girl; you picked a good one."

True, but she liked to hear it at the same time, even if he only said that because she was a guest. Blake handed Sadie a wafer of oatmeal and sweet molasses smelling delicious enough to eat. "Thank you," she managed. Sadie held the treat flat in her hand and let Sunny's soft muzzle and whiskers tickle her palm nibbling the sweet homemade treat. The mare's deep brown eyes topped with gold-colored eyelashes said nothing about fearing this place.

"May I go in?" she asked.

"Sure, since you know what to do around horses. We don't let guests back here or let them mess with the horses because most of them think they know more than they do. But don't tell anyone I said that, okay?" He winked at her.

Maybe he wasn't so bad after all. He opened the massive stall door, and Sadie noticed the pristine state of the stable including stall bars clean of cobwebs, crisp sawdust for bedding, hay hung in hay nets, and water buckets spic and span. The barn smelled of fresh-cut grassy hay. She entered the stall and ran her hands along Sunny's neck. Sunny turned to her, and Sadie convinced herself the mare recognized her. Mom always said animals remembered who rescued them.

Sadie continued to pet Sunny along the length of her body and marveled at how far she had come since the auction. Back then, she was covered in filth and grime. Her mane and tail were so matted and dirty they were mousey brown rather than blondish white. The mare filled out nicely, no more ribs and hip bones sticking out. Sunny's eyes were desperate then, not like now. Sadie asked, "How's she working out here? I mean, other than being lame yesterday."

"She's been solid. We're never sure how rescue horses are going to work out because some do, and some don't. The ranch buys a handful every year to help out the rescues. We all thought it was crazy to get one all the way from Maryland. But the boss wanted her, and he's usually right."

"What was it about Sunny that made him want her?" Dumb, Sadie, why don't you ask Mr. Mac?

"He said she had a kind eye. And she's young enough at seven to have a long life ahead of her but not so young she likes to cause people trouble."

"How is she to ride?"

"You'll find out tomorrow. We already had you on her."

Why did he wait this long to tell her this? "You think she's going to be okay?"

"What I think doesn't matter, it's what the vet thinks," he said. "Dr. Graham said she'll be fine. You know how it goes. Sometimes they're off, and we're not sure why. Could be they stepped wrong or got into mischief with each other when we turned them loose for the night. She'll be fresh and fit for you in the morning."

Sadie gave Sunny one more pat, pulled her cell phone out, and took a selfie of the two of them. She didn't care if Blake thought that was cute or not. She was here for a reason.

CHAPTER 8

⌐

THE HAT

SADIE WALKED TO GRANDMA'S cabin up the dirt path past her family's cabin. She focused on the surroundings to take her mind off of the condescending Blake. She wondered if there was a rule stating she shouldn't have been in the barn or if he was showing her that he was in control. She told herself to stop thinking about it.

Admiring the natural habitat and presence of wildlife everywhere, she took in the squirrels skittering up trees, and insects humming. Birds chirped, and frogs croaked. These same critters lived in Maryland, but they sounded different here with the surrounding quiet accentuating every sound. She swore she heard a squirrel chewing a nut.

The wood-burned engraved sign above the log cabin's door read "Helena." As Sadie reached to knock, Grandma startled her by swinging the door open.

"I thought you'd be here! I'm surprised you took so

long. I can't wait to show you around." Grandma grabbed her by the hand and pulled her across the threshold into her home for the week. "I feel like a pioneer woman."

The pinewood scent combined with some spice warmed her insides. A different set of paintings adorned the walls depicting scenes of cowboys, horses, cattle, covered wagons, and settlers. An overstuffed chair similar to the one in the Kalispell cabin sat in the corner facing the flat screen TV. That picture alone confirmed the guests were only pioneers in their own minds.

"It's nice, Grandma, and all to yourself. I hope some outlaw doesn't try to come get you," Sadie teased.

"Don't you worry about me. I can take care of myself. Did I tell you I've been taking jujitsu?"

"Yes, and I was kidding. This doesn't seem like a place outlaws would come to, even back in the old days. I think they liked to rob people on the move, like settlers, and stagecoaches, and people on trains. I suspect the people at resorts were okay."

"Just in case, I'm prepared. Besides, come in here." Sadie followed her to a second room, the bedroom. "A spare bed, so we can be bunkmates some night if we hear there're outlaws on the loose."

"Why wait for outlaws to do that? We can do it for fun and stay up late like we used to. But guess what? I got to see Sunny!" She showed Grandma the picture on her phone. "And I'm going to ride her tomorrow!"

"How wonderful! She looks fit as a fiddle, and how exciting about riding her. I'll bet you can't wait."

She was excited, and — nervous?

Grandma continued, "I'm glad you came because I have a surprise for you!" She reached into her suitcase and pulled out a sizable square box.

"That filled up half your suitcase."

"It did, which is why I brought two. Don't you kids feel bad about teasing me now?" Grandma fiddled with the box and placed it on her bed. "Open it. I couldn't wrap it because of security."

Sadie took the lid off the box and removed a tasteful brown cowboy hat with a brown, black, and white hat band. "Wow, I don't know what to say."

"Thank you will do. But I need to tell you about it. The band is made of braided horse hair, and I chose the one with Lucky's colors. That way, it's like he's right here with you."

Turning the hat around and touching the thick felt of the brim Sadie said, "You're right, Lucky's colors, and the tassel on the end reminds me of his tail."

"I knew it would. You saw what people are wearing here, didn't you? You don't want to stand out like some teenager from the East Coast, do you?" She smiled, making creases in the corners of her eyes.

"I love it. Thank you. And I love yours, too. They almost look alike."

"I know, but I didn't want them to look exactly alike because I didn't want anyone confusing us." Grandma had such a sense of humor. Sadie was dark, like her dad, but with her mom's freckles. Grandma was blonde, fair skinned, with sky blue eyes.

Sadie donned her new hat, and Grandma fussed around, bending the brim, adjusting. "There, now you can see." She moved her around to face the horn-rimmed mirror on top of her burlwood dresser.

She looked like a real cowgirl. "I don't mind this look," Sadie said, unusual considering she found fault with the way she looked most of the time lately.

"Don't mind? You're stunning! The colors in that band bring out your dark brown eyes. You're prettier every year, and you look like a movie star from one of the classic Westerns."

"I guess you do, too, since you had to buy us different hats so people could tell us apart," Sadie said with a grin.

"Come on, it has to be time for supper. Time to see who else is at this place. Could be I'll find a new husband."

"Grandma!"

"Oh, so you're the only one who can joke around here?"

Grandma put her arm around Sadie's shoulder, and Sadie got a whiff of her signature perfume, Yellow Tea Rose. An appropriate choice for Grandma since she was lovely inside and out. But if someone crossed her or her family, she could use her thorns.

—

CHAPTER 9

RANCH-STYLE SUPPER

Sadie and Grandma chatted on the way to meet the rest of the family. They joined the Navarros on their porch in the two open rocking chairs. Mom and Dad sat on a glider, and Austin in a low Adirondack chair doing something with his phone. He'd be lost without connectivity.

"Let's go; they're not going to hold the chuck wagon for us," Grandma said.

Austin raised his head from his phone and said, "I don't remember Mr. Mac saying anything about a chuck wagon. He said to be at dinner, I mean, 'supper' at six o'clock. It's only five-thirty and a five-minute walk at most."

"There you go with details again. I have the smartest

grandkids, don't you think?" Grandma searched in Mom and Dad's direction for confirmation.

"Can't disagree with you," Dad said. "What do you two think of our view? It might as well be in a travel brochure."

The porch faced a mountain range with a stream running below. Cattle grazed in grass pastures the color of a green Crayola crayon. The sun receded leaving an array of pastel lines and colors stretching for miles.

"I could get used to this," Grandma said.

"Me, too," Dad said.

"Wait until the winter," Austin said. "Where'd you get the hat, cowgirl?"

Sadie nodded toward Grandma and said, "Where do you think?"

"Yeah, you're Grandma's favorite."

"Not true! I love you each in your own way. You might not remember this, young man, but I'm the one who gave you your cowboy hat back when you lived in California. You took care of it over the years, and you look as handsome in that hat as Sadie is in hers. Your grandmother knows how to shop."

"I like the hat," Dad said. "I don't think I've ever seen you in one of those. It makes you look…older."

"Thanks, Dad, I think."

Mom got up and walked over to Sadie. She reached

down and adjusted the brim like her own mother had done to her not long ago. "You blend right in." She mouthed the words "thank you" to Grandma.

"Oh! I haven't had a chance to tell you all, I got to see Sunny! Here, let me show you a picture." She made the rounds with her phone, and everyone commented how different she looked compared to when Sadie first rescued her.

Mom asked, "How did you find her?"

"I saw the horses on our way to the cabin and figured she'd be there. She was." Sadie didn't tell them the full story.

"Mission accomplished. Let's change step and move out," Dad said. He used a lot of Navy talk, and he'd done it so long the whole family spoke Navy. That was his way of saying, "Let's go."

"I'm going to wash my hands real quick, and I suggest everyone else do the same," Mom said.

"Yes, ma'am," Dad saluted. He could be a jester like her brother.

They may be in a place like none of them had been before, but some things didn't change. Dad liked to give orders; Mom always had the final say. Austin stayed chill, and Grandma was full of surprises. Sadie loved horses, and that's why they were all there.

They headed for the main lodge. She noticed other

guests finding their way to dinner looking like it was their first time as well.

When they entered the hall, a young woman in a tan cowboy hat and a red bandanna around her neck said, "Welcome, and yes, you're in the right place. Please find a seat anywhere you'd like, and we'll get started soon."

Ten chairs sat at each of the round pinewood tables covered with red-checkered tablecloths. Pitchers of water and iced tea occupied a lazy susan in the middle of each table so guests could twirl the beverages close to them. The spinning server also had condiments like salt, pepper, sugar, creamer, ketchup, mustard, and hot sauce. Wagon wheel chandeliers hung above them contributing to the ranch atmosphere.

Mom said, "How about here?" She pointed to an empty table not far from the front door. No one objected, so they took their seats. Beef brisket, fried potatoes, and cornbread aromas filled the room causing Sadie's stomach to growl.

"Was that you?" Austin asked, sitting next to her.

"Yeah, I guess I'm hungrier than I thought. It must be the fresh air." Fellow ranch guests filed into the room. Sadie and Austin had a game they'd played for years where they made up stories about people. That would be fun here.

People chatted and laughed and meandered around

reminding Sadie of awkward scenes in school lunchrooms. She'd done it herself enough times as the new kid in school looking for a friendly face or a place to sit where someone might welcome her. She wondered what it would be like to have friendships lasting for ten years instead of two or three, depending on how long her dad was stationed somewhere. Her brother was her only true long-term friend.

"Are these seats taken?" a woman asked with a slight European accent.

"Only these five," Dad answered. "Please join us." Dad was friendly and sociable, and he would know everyone at the ranch by the time they left.

"*Grazie,*" the woman said, and herded a man of the same age and a young girl around the table. "Tony, you sit next to the lady. We sit boy-girl, boy-girl, but more girls than boys, so we'll have to make do." She broke the ice, and everyone smiled.

Mom turned to the gentleman and said, "Hi, I'm Liz, and this is my husband, Jim, my mother, Anna, son, Austin, and daughter, Sadie. It's a pleasure to meet you."

He nodded and turned to his female companion. "My husband, he doesn't speak much English. He understands, but you know, proud Italian man." She rubbed the top of his hand on the table. "Allow me, I'm Regina, this is my husband, Tony, or Mrs. and Mr. DiLeonardi for the children, and our daughter Pamela." She pronounced it Pa-MAY-la similar to the Spanish pronunciation of Pa-MEY-la.

Pamela eyed Austin and Sadie. "Mama, they're not children. They're teenagers, like me."

Sadie already liked her. She spoke good English and had a certain spark to her. Sadie said, "Is it okay if Pamela sits over here with us? We don't want to holler across the table or anything."

"Go on and play, *bambina*, enough adults for you today," her mother said.

Pamela turned to Sadie and rolled her eyes; it must be an international expression. Her shiny black hair fell in waves down to her elbows. She scooted over two seats and said, "*Buongiorno*, I'm happy to see other people here my age. I thought it would be all old people and little kids."

"You and me both," Austin said. "So where you from? We're from Maryland."

"Oh, Maryland!" She said it that funny way some people do who are not from Maryland. Marylanders said the state as a two-syllable word: Mareland. Many others would annunciate each syllable as Mar-y-land. "I know of Maryland and the Thoroughbred horses and racing. How exciting! And I'm from Italy, Napoli, or as you say, Naples." She made a face like tasting a sour candy.

"We went there when our dad was stationed in Spain,"

Austin said, as if everyone had. "We got to travel a bit in Europe. The food was the best." He elbowed Sadie and said, "This one here was in her fried chicken phase so missed a lot of it. But she was brave enough to try the pizza."

Sadie wasn't sure why he had to tell that story, but that's how brothers were sometimes. She asked, "Do you ride much, and have you ever been to a ranch?"

"I've taken dressage lessons for six years, so not like your Western riding. But I think I can hang on. And no, no ranches. This was my papa's dream, to ride like a cowboy in the Wild West." Pamela looked in her father's direction. "See how ready he is, and he hasn't been near a horse yet!"

"We're here because of Sadie," Austin said. "But so far it seems like we're going to have a good time."

Five tables were mostly full, and workers bustled around the outskirts of the room setting large pans of food in silver-covered buffet dishes. They placed stacks of plates at one end and silverware on the other. A cooler of canned refreshments sat at the end. These folks could teach the folks at the school cafeteria a thing or two about how to feed people.

Mr. Mac stood by the buffet table and spoke into a portable microphone like the ones riding instructors used. "Can I have your attention, please?" The discussions among new friends at the tables died down. "First and foremost, welcome again to Homeplace Ranch. We call it this because it's how we want you to feel for the week, like you are at home here. Our goal is to help people enjoy the ranch life we've been blessed to have and continue our family's ranching legacy. We hope you found everything you needed so far, and I'll get into more of what's in store for you this week after supper.

"I don't want to hold you up any longer, so let's start with this table here and wind our way around the room. Enjoy the meal our fine kitchen staff, led by my darlin' Keela, has put together for you tonight. Everything's labeled, so don't you worry, no mystery meat here." Small laughs erupted, and Sadie thought Mr. Mac must like his job of being a ranch owner and an entertainer.

CHAPTER 10

PLANS FOR THE WEEK

SADIE DEVOURED HER HOME-COOKED hearty meal of mostly meat and potatoes. If she ate like this all week, new jeans would be in order.

She, Austin, and Pamela talked throughout the meal finding out more about each other. Pamela studied English since the first grade and was now fifteen. She said, "I wanted to know what those words of American songs meant."

Dad spoke to Mr. DiLeonardi in Spanish since Dad didn't speak Italian, and Mr. DiLeonardi didn't care to speak English. Somehow the two communicated. They gestured and got louder as people sometimes do when they are trying to understand another person with a language barrier between them. Watching the laughing and interactions around the table, Sadie didn't feel as bad for dragging her family here.

Kitchen staff and wranglers dressed in jeans, boots, and button-down plaid, checkered, and plain-colored shirts came by and cleared off the tables. Sadie recognized a few of the wranglers from the corral. She hoped she didn't run into that Blake wrangler again anytime soon. As soon as the dishes cleared, the same people showed up with trays of desserts and pots of coffee for the guests.

Pamela said, "Espresso?" to a handsome wrangler.

"Not here, but this isn't too bad. Try it." She nodded, and he poured her a steaming cup that smelled like stale mud to Sadie. She didn't like coffee or any form of it. Pamela blew on her coffee and took a small sip. She licked her lips like a cat, so sophisticated for her age. She blinked and smiled to the young wrangler who registered her appreciation and continued around the table pouring coffee for those interested. He looked more like he should be handling saddles than serving coffee.

Mr. Mac moved to the front of the room and addressed the guests: "I hope you had enough to eat, and while you're having your dessert, I'll tell you about the upcoming week. You ready?"

Spirited yeahs and yeehas resounded from the crowd. "First, let's talk about who's here. How many of you noticed the flagpole with multiple flags out front when you pulled up?" His eyes moved from table to table; several heads nodded. "Those flags represent where you all are from. This week we are joined by Americans, Italians, Australians, and Canadians."

A group of women at a table whooped it up, and the oldest one shouted out, "That's us, in case ya hadn't figured it out!" They would be fun.

"There's forty of you total, which is a big group. Don't worry, we don't do any nose-to-tail riding out here, and we won't all be going out in one group. We'll split you up in two basic groups and mix it up once in a while based on the kinds of rides you want to do. We offer plenty of time in the saddle, and hopefully you will learn to love the ranch lifestyle."

"I run a clinic the day after tomorrow for those who want to brush up on their Western riding skills."

"It's excellent," an older female guest with a southern accent hollered. "I did it last year and recommend it. In fact, I'm doing it again."

"Thank you, Debbie. Debbie here is what we call a three-timer, meaning her third trip to our ranch."

Pamela covered her mouth and whispered to Sadie, "Want to go?"

Sadie nodded. It was decided then and there.

Mr. Mac continued, making eye contact with the guests: "As many of you know, we offer more than riding here. We have hiking trails, bikes, and excursions including fly fishing, target shooting, and golf." Dad gave Sadie a thumbs-up as if she had set it all up. Mr. DiLeonardi smiled and pointed to Dad and back to himself, pantomiming the swing of a golf club. He obviously understood the English word golf. The two would be golfing one of the days they were here. So much for the Wild West!

"Each evening we hold an event, so you won't be bored. Our entertainment happens in this room after supper. We're warning you, by the end of the week, *you* are going to be our entertainment. So bring out your cowboy poetry, singing talents, or whatever you've got." What was Sadie's talent? There were forty people there, so she hoped she wasn't one of the performers. She hated being on stage. Days from now, she tucked that concern away for the time being.

"And on Tuesday night, we go into town for the rodeo."

"There's a special Native American crafts workshop one night for those who might want to create their own keepsakes to take home. Every night, our senior wranglers take turns hosting after-hours campfires at Miners Hollow. Don't attend those if you are afraid of ghost stories and ghosts!"

Mr. Mac's eyes sparkled like her Grandma's did. She needed to remember to ask him if he was Irish. "For those of you who came out here to relax, enjoy your comfy cabins … and Wi-Fi. And for the nightlife folks, on Thursday we shuttle you to the best saloon in Utica for live music. The 21-and-older crowd can dance, two-step, and live it up."

"What about us who aren't twenty-one yet?" a girl whined from across the room.

"Tonight's your chance! We take a short break after supper before the entertainment starts. And tonight, our local band, Just Us, will regale you with their music, and we'll teach you line dances. Will that work?"

"You think of everything," she said.

"Been doing this a while, missy. For any of you who head back to your lodging for the night after finishing your desserts, breakfast is at eight every morning, right here. I'll be telling you about ride options for the next day every night, like this, in case you decide to skip breakfast. But I don't advise it! We don't want to hurt Keela's feelings, do we?" The crowd laughed.

"Before we end here, I want to introduce you to the rest of my family and staff since you'll be seeing them all week." He motioned a young man in the back forward. "C'mon, son."

No way. Blake.

"You met my high school sweetheart, Keela, when you checked in, and this is our son, Blake, one of your wranglers." Blake's eyes scanned the room, something he must have practiced weekly. They landed on Sadie, and he tipped his hat.

He tricked her. Why didn't he mention who he was? And now she recognized who he looked like — his father. The anger he'd sparked in her earlier rose again. How insolent.

"Sadie, he likes you," Pamela said in a low voice only Sadie could hear. She wore an impish grin.

"No, he's paid to like people."

Her new Italian friend shook her head "no" and reached over and patted Sadie's thigh. Sadie remembered her Spanish friends being touchy-feely, too, so she was used to it.

Mr. Mac continued introducing his family which included two daughters older than Blake. They joined Mr. Mac where he stood. "This is my oldest, Sierra, and she's a wrangler." She was the girl who greeted the Navarros at the door for dinner. "And this is Morgan, who helps Keela with everything."

"We can't do it all, so we have folks who've been with us for a long time. They're like family to us." He pointed to the opposite side of the room where a group of older cowboys stood. "Meet Rusty, Levi, Cody, and Joe." They each raised their hand and waved after he called their name.

"Finally, our ranch hands over here will be helping you this week." He gestured with his arm toward the right side of the room. "Luke is in charge," the oldest one waved, younger than the wranglers he just introduced, maybe mid-twenties. "And we've got Miss Kitty, Justin, Doug, Carlos, and Cash." They appeared to be about Austin's age. She recognized one of them as the coffee guy. "They haven't been here as long, but they keep the machine oiled and the horses taken care of.

"I'm gonna let you go before the band sets up, but we'll be here during the break to answer questions. Please ask any of our team; we're all here to help you have a good time."

Sadie wanted to get out of there. "Mom, can I go check on Sunny?"

"Sure, and maybe Pamela wants to go." Mom turned to Mrs. DiLeonardi, "Would that be okay?"

"Not a problem," she answered. "Don't forget to come back, sweetheart."

"Austin, do you want to go?" Sadie asked.

"Not really; I'll see horses all week. I'm going to stretch my legs, meet some folks, and take some pictures. We're only here for a week."

Sadie stood up, and Pamela did the same, saying, "*Scuzi*," to the people at the table. Sadie beelined to the door, with Pamela following. Outside, the cooler temperature chilled her, and Sadie made a mental note to dress warm at night around here.

"What's the rush? You Americans, always in such a hurry."

She didn't want to explain her encounter with Blake as they walked and talked. "Did I tell you about Sunny?"

"No, your brother did, and what a story! I would hope to rescue horses someday. You must be so proud! And getting to see her again? I should have asked before, but where are we going?"

Sadie answered, "To the red barn next to the corral over there; we're almost there." Sadie reached the barn door she entered not long ago, and found it shut for the evening. She knew she wasn't supposed to be here on her own, but could it be so bad to peek in?

She slid the door open, knowing it wouldn't be locked because that would be unsafe for the horses inside in case something happened. It was darker than before and nickers greeted the door opening. Horses munched hay and something sounding like a cat jumped down from above with a thud.

Sadie peered through the door at the third stall looking for movement. She called out, "Sunny, it's me, and I brought a friend. Can you poke your head out and say hi?"

Nothing.

Sadie took a step inside and heard Blake's words in her

mind about guests not being allowed. She took another step, and Pamela followed. "Um, we're not supposed to be in here, but I thought we'd be able to see her from the door. You can wait outside if you want."

"No, I'm with you." She smiled.

Empty stall. Where did she go? Oh, boy, Sadie had only been here six hours and had already lost the horse she came to see who had been standing here in this stall.

A male voice rang out by the door. "Can I help you?"

She dreaded turning around but did. It was the coffee guy Mr. Mac had introduced as Justin. "She's gone!"

"You mean the new mare?"

She had a lump in her throat so nodded instead.

"She's at the top field. Instructions said she was ready to go, so we let her out with the others. I'm here to check on the four horses still here."

"So Sunny's okay?"

"She's fine, and probably happier. None of them like being stuck in their stalls; they want to be free and with their herd."

Sadie liked the way he talked about horses like he understood their feelings. "Sorry, I've been rude, but I was so worried about her that it cluttered my brain. I'm Sadie, and this is Pamela."

"Justin. How do you know Sunny?"

"It's a long story, and you're working. Thanks for

telling me she's safe. We'll be going; sorry for holding you up." Why did she keep apologizing?

Pamela said, "She rescued her!" Oh, brother, everyone in Montana would know before long at this rate.

He studied her. "That was the right thing to do. Let's talk later — sounds like a good story. I'll get back to my chores, so I can get back to our camp. Sunrise comes early. Pardon me, and nice to meet you both."

What a different encounter than earlier. He didn't insult her, leave out important details of who he was, or tell her she couldn't be in the barn. She had jumped to conclusions about Sunny being missing, and he didn't tease her about that. Sunny was fine, and she already had a new Italian friend and a cowboy who'd been nice to her. Things were looking up.

CHAPTER 11

A CHANCE TO RIDE

BREAKFAST COULDN'T BE OVER fast enough. Ready to ride, Sadie tapped her foot under the table while everyone chatted about the band and dancing last night, and the good time had by all. This morning the five Canadian women joined them at their table with their animated conversation and laughter. It turned out these horsewomen had gathered for an all-girls vacation each year for the past ten years, each time to a different spot.

Pamela waved at Sadie from across the room, and she waved back. Sadie hoped they would be on the same ride today, but she wasn't sure how that worked. Mr. Mac stood at his place in front of the room and addressed the group again. He asked who was going on what non-riding excursions and assigned people in different directions.

Once done with that, he said, "So I'll bet the rest of you are riding today." The crowd responded enthusiastically. "Let's step outside, set you up for the day, and match you up with your partners. As some of you may have seen, we offer mules, too, for those who prefer those sure-footed mounts."

One of the Canadians said to her friends, "Mule for me for sure. I can ride a horse any day." Sadie didn't understand why anyone would want to ride anything other than a horse, but she didn't know much about mules.

He continued, "This first ride will be an easy one so you can all get acquainted with your animals. The easy start also helps those of you who don't ride as much get used to the riding. We'll split you into two groups, based on the people you came with. C'mon, let's go."

They assembled outside the corral filled with horses all tacked up and ready and tied along the rails. Someone had done all the work. Sadie knew how much effort it was to tack up one horse, and there were about thirty horses and mules ready. She recalled what Justin said about sunrise coming early. The horses stood lazily waiting on humans. Sadie spotted Sunny and wanted to run over and hug her but contained herself.

"Oh, I want *that* one!" the smallest girl there squealed, pointing to a snowy-white pony.

Mr. Mac said, "We'll sort all that out soon. First, let me figure out who is in which group."

"Why?" she asked, her mother grabbing her hand to quiet her.

"No problem, ma'am. Remember, I encouraged people to ask questions. What's your name, little one?"

"Brittany."

"Brittany, the answer to your question is it has to do with the horses and mules. You see, horses are herd animals, and like us, they make friends. We don't want to separate the friends, do we?"

Brittany shook her head no.

Mr. Mac divided the group into two, and the Navarros and DiLeonardis would ride together. Sadie and Pamela gave each other the thumbs-up sign, apparently another universal signal. Austin wandered around taking pictures to send to Katie. This all took too long.

"Okay, folks, come see Blake, Sierra, Luke, Justin, Cody, Joe, and me, so we can get you set up with the right horse, mule, or pony for you."

Blake announced, "We brought these horses and mules based on the questions you answered on your applications about your size and riding capabilities. We try to match it right, but we want to make sure it works out for you."

"Of course he got it right," Sadie whispered to Pamela standing next to her.

"I don't know why you don't like him. I think he's the image of a handsome young American cowboy, like the ones in the paintings around here."

"He's all yours, then," Sadie said and resumed listening to Mr. Mac's instructions.

"Come on up, don't be shy, one of us will set you up." Mr. Mac gestured the guests forward.

Sadie approached Sierra. "Hi, I'm Sadie, and I'm supposed to ride Sunny today."

"Nice to meet you, Sadie." They must repeat people's names to remember them for the week. One obviously needed to acquire certain skills to be successful in the hospitality business. "Let's go; she's right over here."

Sadie smiled at her and said, "I know; I saw her. It's nice to meet you, too."

As they walked over to Sunny, Sierra said in a warm, friendly tone, "I heard your story, and how you've made quite a trip to check on a horse. That's honorable."

Honorable? She sure thought different than her brother. Sadie said, "It's important for the rescues. And I feel an obligation to her."

"I understand. I'd want to know. I think you're going to find she has a great life out here with us. Here she is."

Sierra untied the halter and slipped it off leaving the

headstall and reins on. She backed her up and turned her away from the other horses and mules still tied. "Did you ride her before she came here?"

"No, this will be my first time. But I own a horse and ride as much as I can."

"Dad said you could ride. Sunny's a nice ride. I worked with her when she first got here. She's smart and wants to please."

Sadie beamed. "Do you want me to get on here?"

"No, let's use one of the mounting blocks." She led Sunny to one of the five mounting blocks they had staged in appropriate places to make it easier for the "dudes" to mount their horses and mules. Sadie swung her leg over Sunny and felt at home. The stirrups hung at exactly the right length.

"Everything okay?" Sierra asked.

Sadie nodded.

"Okay, I'll lead you out and ask you to stay in the area we're going to while we help the others. See you soon since I'm one of your group's wranglers today."

A girl wrangler, how lucky to have that job. Sadie walked Sunny slowly feeling her movement and getting used to the ranch's tack. The mare's wide Quarter Horse body felt comfortable beneath her and different from Lucky's leaner build. At 15.2 hands high, Sunny sat four inches shorter than Lucky, which didn't seem like it would make much of a difference, but it did. Sadie scratched the mare's withers and listened to the surrounding banter.

One of the guests had never ridden — never! Wrangler Joe set him up with Fred, a mule whose mother, or dam, had been a Belgian draft horse. Fred's reddish tan coat shone in the sun, and his legs, tail, and mane were cream-colored. He had a white nose, and white hairs around his eyes. He was adorable and reminded Sadie of Goliath, the Belgian draft horse she saved, a favorite therapy horse at Maryland Therapeutic Riding.

Brittany and her mother approached Sierra, who pointed to the white pony and said to the girl, "You like her, huh? And look at that, she's just your size." She led them to the pony. "This here is Abby, named for the white stone, abalone. I picked her out for you to ride."

Brittany shrieked, and heads turned in her direction. Sadie hoped she'd never shrieked like that, even at that girl's age. But she couldn't help but enjoy seeing her excitement.

She overheard Grandma saying, "Mac, I want a sensible horse. And one low to the ground for when I jump back on out on the ponderosa."

"Anna, I've been thinking about the right match for you since we first talked. Meet Sweetie."

Sadie positioned herself so she had a better view. Sweetie looked over her shoulder at Grandma showing her full flaxen mane in contrast to her deep sorrel body. Chubby Sweetie, the color of a copper penny, did not appear to be the one to take off in a spirited gallop for no reason.

"You know how to pick them, Mac, like I do," Grandma said. She strode in front of Sweetie in her teal cowboy boots and studied her eyes. She stroked her forehead and said, "You and I are going to get along fine, Sweetie; I can tell."

Mr. Mac helped Grandma step onto Sweetie, and Sadie was proud of her grandmother who mounted the horse with grace. It may have been her riding lessons, her surfing, or her jujitsu, but Grandma got on that horse better than most of those Sadie had seen here. Mr. Mac asked her about her stirrups and her comfort and made simple adjustments.

"Grandma, over here!" Sadie called.

"On my way," she answered. "As long as it's okay with Mac."

"Go on. Glad you like your horse. She's a former polo pony with a sound mind. She's athletic and won't spook at a thing. Kinda reminds me of you now that I've met you in person." He winked at her.

Grandma joined Sadie, and Mr. Mac went off to work his next horse-to-human matchmaking.

"What do you think?" Grandma asked.

"How cool — a polo pony! And what a looker."

"I don't care as much about that; I want a steady mind. I like that in people, too," Grandma laughed. "So this is Sunny? I only heard about her and didn't meet her during the whole adoption evolution, except in pictures. She's come a long way from what I remember seeing back then. She's beautiful."

Mom, Dad, and Austin met up with them on their equine partners as they joined up. It was obvious to Sadie Homeplace Ranch trained their horses well because everyone behaved. It dawned on Sadie that people like the rest of her family who knew less about horses than she did were more relaxed on them. They weren't expecting bad behavior. She wished she could be more like that.

CHAPTER 12

ON THE ROAD

THE MATCHMAKING EVENT ENDED, with everyone mounted and headed on their way in their respective groups. Mr. Mac dubbed Sadie's group the Good Guys, and the other group, the Bad Guys. The older wrangler, Joe, led the Good Guys out. He was tall, thin, weathered, and about her dad's age. He looked like a famous Western movie actor with a long white mustache whose name Sadie didn't remember, and he likely had no idea of the resemblance.

Joe rode in the lead and also looked backwards to check on everyone. That was a skill in itself in this terrain and showed his leadership and experience. Sierra and Justin assisted him with the fifteen guests on this ride, with Justin as the only ranch hand on the ride. Did this mean he was a wrangler-in-training? And why did she care? Because in the short time she knew Justin, he cared about horses, and she liked people who cared about horses.

When they were ten minutes out, Joe turned around and announced, "We're going to take a short break here." They were on a flat bluff with room for the group to spread out.

What? Already? Sadie tried not to show her impatience.

"Let's gather round here." He waited until all riders came to a stop in a semi-circle in front of him. Sierra and Justin hopped off and tied their horses to a waist-high tree branch.

"First of all, everybody comfortable? Stirrups too long or too short? If so, raise your hands, and Sierra or Justin will help you out. I wanted to explain signals we all use for rides this week. When I raise my right hand like this, it means I'm slowing down and will be stopping. When I point down, like this, it means I'm pointing something out to you, like a broken branch or a hole. When we're riding single file, pass that signal back the line so the people behind you understand. And if I put my arm out like this," he demonstrated by putting his arm straight out from the shoulder with this palm back, "it means you're in trouble." The group laughed.

"We like to get into trouble," one of the Canadian women said.

"Not with me you don't," he joked. "But seriously, no matter the ride, your head wrangler must be in the lead. We know where we're going and how to keep you safe. So this signal," he pointed straight out again, "means stay behind me. So far, we've all been in a line, but as Mac said last night, we won't always ride that way. It's one of the things we take pride in here. We want you to spread out and talk among yourselves. Enjoy the people you're with on the ride or make new friends."

Sadie's eyes connected with Pamela's.

"Remember to stay one horse-length away from the person in front of you and don't crowd each other when riding side-by-side. Be sure to tell one of us if you are having problems, so we can help," Joe said.

Justin appeared out of nowhere standing by Sadie's leg. "Hi again."

"Hi." Sadie focused on the instructions so much she missed him coming.

He said, "Sierra and I are checking cinches — part of our routine at the first stop."

"Oh, thanks, and thanks for helping me last night. I'm not sure what I was thinking."

He checked her cinch, pulled it up a notch, and said, "No, you're good. I understand why you care." He headed back to his horse. She hoped wrangler Joe didn't say anything important because she hadn't heard a word.

He continued, "We'll be spreading out up ahead. Sierra, Justin, all set?"

They were both untying their horses and answered yes. They hopped on, and Joe said, "Let's ride."

Riding up long grassy slopes, hills covered with fir trees appeared in the distance. Everything spread out in front of the group, green and plush under the bright blue sky without a cloud in sight. Beyond the closest hills, mountains shot straight up in the background. The undeveloped land spanned for miles and miles forming a spectacular sight.

The Good Guys spread out, and Sadie expected her mom and dad to head toward her.

Instead, they met up with the DiLeonardis. Mr. DiLeonardi glowed. When her parents had company, Pamela steered her lovely buckskin in next to Sadie. Grandma decided to befriend the Canadian ladies, and Austin followed her.

"Isn't this magnificent?" Pamela asked. "Our countryside has rolling hills, but nothing like this, so big, so open."

"Yes, it is. And how's your horse, I mean, that's why we're here, right?"

"I love him and want to take him home. His name is Tanner, and he's one of your American Quarter Horses, quite popular in Europe."

"They are here, too! I'm loving Sunny, but ssh, don't let my Lucky know. Don't want to hurt his feelings."

"Your secret is safe with me. So, tell me, is this everything you thought it would be?"

"And more. I was so focused on coming to check on this girl here," she touched Sunny's warm neck, "I didn't think much about the fun part. I saw it as something I had to do. Sure, coming to a ranch sounded exciting, but I might as well share another secret with you."

Pamela turned to Sadie and made a motion like she was zipping her own mouth shut. "Safe with me."

"I was worried. I was worried the people here might be offended I thought I needed to check on her. I was worried I might find something bad. I was worried about not knowing what to do."

"And look, all that worry for nothing. Here you are, enjoying the outdoors, meeting new friends, meeting young cowboys," Pamela said.

There she went with the boys again. "I wanted to ask, you said you've studied English for a long time. But why do you speak it so well? I mean, I studied Spanish, lived in Spain, and went to a Spanish school. But my Spanish isn't anything like your English."

"Now it's my turn to share a secret. I watch your American soap operas! Think about it, with all the drama, so easy to tell what's going on. And they don't use complicated words. If you want to speak better, tune in to Spanish novellas. That's my tip of the day." They both laughed.

That explained Pamela's interest in romance.

"My friend, I would love to stay and chat all day, but I need to head back to my family for a while. After all, they paid for me to be here. *Ciao* for now!" Pamela made her way back to where the four parents rode together. She rode with elegance, straight spine, shoulders back, and appeared as comfortable on a ranch horse as she probably did on a fancy dressage horse.

"Having fun, yet?" Sadie turned to her left, noticing Justin's green eyes for the first time.

"Yes, lots." He made her nervous.

"How do you like Sunny?"

"A lot." There's that word again. "She's nice and thick and so sure-footed. We've only walked, but I can't wait to feel her other gaits."

"We'll do some jogging today, for those who want to. We'll break up the group into those who do, and those who don't. Mr. Mac's a planner and figured out ways people of different riding levels can ride together." Justin spoke about Mr. Mac like a father figure.

"That'll be good. Will I get to canter her?"

"You'll be able to lope her if you go on the afternoon ride. The afternoon rides tend to be smaller, and more of our dedicated riders go on those rides. For the ones who hardly ride, one ride a day is enough," he said, scanning the riders ahead.

"I want to ride every chance I have."

"I figured you would be one of those dedicated riders. Anyone who'd come more than halfway across the country to check on a horse she's never ridden must be a true horse lover. I'll see you this afternoon then." He smiled, tipped his hat, and rode off to be friendly with another guest.

The snorts of horses and jingling of saddle parts soothed Sadie while she had time to think of nothing. For the first time in months, she was at peace.

⟿

CHAPTER 13

HORSEKEEPER CONNECT

SADIE HAD TEXTED BRADY pictures of Montana yesterday and today, but she was trying not to show off too much. Deep inside, she knew he wished he were with her on the adventure. She had figured out the time difference between Montana and Maryland and set up a decent time to have a video chat with Brady today.

He answered right away. "Horsekeeper here."

She missed his humor. "How are you?" Seeing the barn background, her heart raced. She hadn't asked him to be there, trying not to put too much on a friend who was already doing her a favor.

"Awesome! First, let me tell you about Lucky. He seems to be missing you, but I keep him company as much as I can."

"I'm sure you are. So, what's awesome?"

"I have a new friend! Her name is Hope, and she's my age. She's been helping me keep Lucky company."

Sadie tried not to let her face twist up on the video call. She was protective of her Lucky. She was being irrational. "I know Hope. Didn't she tell you? We've ridden together."

"Oh, she told me. Hold on, we're both here. Follow me." He held the phone behind his head, creating a blurry and out-of-focus trip down the barn aisle. She loved him for his well-intended theatrics.

"Hope," he called, "I'm bringing you Sadie all the way from Montana!"

The young girl emerged from Robin's stall, waving at the phone. "Lucky's mom! Hello again. I love Lucky! He's being such a good boy."

"Hi there and thank you for helping Brady with him — not that he needs any help."

"Let's go visit Lucky, while we're all here," Brady said and walked away with the phone behind him. Hope took the phone from him to assist as they moved down the aisle. Most of the horses were inside during the day for the summer to keep them out of the heat. The barn workers turned them out at night to graze and live with their herds of friends.

Hope narrated, "Here's Finn, say hello." She zoomed

in on Finn, a young Thoroughbred owned by a seven-teen-year-old boarder, Hannah. "And here's Thor. Brady told me all about you and Thor and how you rescued each other. What a story!"

Sadie listened and thought of how in the short time she knew Hope, the girl knew more about her than people she had known for much longer.

"Hi, Thor," Hope continued. "I'm not sure how many times you've talked into a phone, so I hope it makes sense to you." Hope stroked Thor in a way displaying her admiration of the gray draft horse cross. Then she turned the camera to herself and said, "Okay, I think he's fine. Let's go find Brady and Lucky."

Hope focused the phone ahead toward Lucky's stall. When she arrived, Brady popped up and said, "Ta da!" like a magician.

Seeing Lucky took her breath away as usual. As nice as the Homeplace Ranch horses were, none were close to him. Guilt filled her for enjoying the other horses while she neglected her own. Lucky's face quickly filled the phone's screen with the handy work of her cameramen on the ground.

Sadie leaned into her phone and spoke, "Lucky Boy, do you miss me? You would love this place. I tell everyone about you. And in case I miss anyone, Grandma makes sure to tell them about you." She felt juvenile talking to a horse thinking he might understand. This seemed like something a kid would do, not someone of her age.

Lucky poked the phone with his nose as he had done in the past. Please don't disconnect us! She teared up, glad no one else could see. He looked straight into her eyes and into her soul. How did he do that?

"Sadie ... are you there?" Hope asked.

"She's fine," Brady said. "Lucky has a way of making people feel better without talking. Let's give her a minute. Hope fiddled with the phone, and the screen rocked and moved around and then stopped. "Hope set up the phone so you could talk to Lucky alone. She knows a lot more about these phone things, and well, everything, than I do."

"Don't pick on yourself; I hate it when you do that. You both have different talents."

Lucky neighed, interrupting the friendship conversation. "Sorry, Lucky."

"We'll be back," Brady said.

Sadie's voice got low, and she spoke to Lucky in their special Sadie-Lucky language made up of things like "Ch-ch, g'boy, aww, and you're the best." She didn't care if she sounded like a kid.

When she stopped speaking and clucking, Hope picked up the phone and handed it to Brady. "I think we've taken good care of him," he said, exuding pride.

"Yes, a blue ribbon for the horsekeeper! Seeing Lucky sure made me miss him."

"He understands you're away, but I think he also understands you left me in charge. As his groom for the horse shows, and someone who's been around him a lot, I can tell he's not lonely. We take him out and walk him and give him exercises to do like we've done before in Miss Kristy's program."

Sadie nodded and looked down. He was doing his best.

Hope said, "I saw the champion ribbon on Lucky's stall — how impressive."

"Thank you, and you and Robin can do that. You have to believe you can."

"I think it will take a lot of work, but why not try?"

"Then you'd better get back to work! If Brady agrees, we can share the same horse show groom. He helped us at all our horse shows, so part of that ribbon is his."

"I'm in," he said. "Before you go, can you please tell us about Sunny?"

Sunny — how could she forget to tell him about why she was there? "You got the pictures, right?"

"Yeah, she's pretty and looks happy," Brady said.

Sadie didn't mention the temporary lameness problem from yesterday. "The people are great here, and she's fitting in well. I got to ride her! And I get to ride her again for this afternoon's ride."

"I'm glad it all worked out!" Brady said, and he smiled the widest smile of the call. "I guess we should go, so you can go do ranch things. Have fun, and don't worry about anything here."

"All right, bye for now then. It's neat here, but I do miss home … and you."

"You'll be back before you know it," Brady said. "Take care!" They ended the call on their end.

The check-in was supposed to make her feel better, but it had the opposite effect. She missed her horse, and the doubts crept back in about whether she was too big for her britches in thinking she understood more about how to treat a rescue horse than these experienced ranchers. She wasn't getting too much right these days.

CHAPTER 14

THE RIVER RIDE

SADIE WAS THE ONLY one in her family to go on the afternoon ride because everyone chose other things to do not involving more saddle time. Sadie understood and liked the independence. Her friend, Pamela, opted for a Western riding lesson at the ranch instead, so Sadie was on her own.

Sadie rode mostly English in Maryland these days, but she still rode Western occasionally and owned a special Western saddle her grandmother had gifted her for last year's birthday. She rode Lucky in that saddle for lessons at Loftmar to prepare for this ride which turned out to be an excellent decision. While others complained about sore legs and other body parts from the morning ride, she had no problems.

Arriving at the corral at the designated two o'clock ride time, Sadie found Sunny dozing on her feet in the afternoon sun waiting for her. Instead of going up to pet her, Sadie let her take the nap she deserved after this morning's ride. Other guests talked among each other and relived moments they'd had so far in the trip.

A brunette with shoulder-length curly hair and a heart-shaped face spoke to Sadie. "This looks like it will be an all-girl ride." Her name was Heather, the youngest of the Canadian women, whom Mr. Mac called the Canadian Five. "I asked for a mule for this one."

"Why?" Sadie asked.

"I can ride a horse anytime. Besides, I like mules; they're sturdy. And there's something about their personalities. I hope I didn't say all this positive stuff about them and curse myself."

"All the horses and mules were good this morning. They must be used to this."

"That, and they've had excellent training," Heather said. "You can tell. How's your horse?"

"Awesome, couldn't be better. She had some training at the rescue before she got here, but she seems to be adapting like a trouper."

"Will your grandmother be joining us? She's a hoot."

"No, she's taking a break. A hoot's about right," Sadie said.

"Oops ... there went the all-girls ride." Mr. Mac marched out of the red barn to meet them in front of the paddock. Justin followed.

Mr. Mac counted heads mouthing the numbers and looked at his watch. He gestured to call the scattered group in closer. There were only nine of them, and Sadie hoped that didn't mean he'd dismiss Justin from the ride.

"This is a small group. I believe you're all experienced riders, right? Give me a nod if yes." His eyes moved from each woman to the next — the five Canadians, a mother and two daughters, and Sadie. Each one nodded her confirmation.

"We kept all your horses and mules for you from this morning, and we pulled some extras. Heather wanted to ride a mule, so I found the orneriest one I could for her." He grinned at her. "Anyone else want to change, or are you comfortable with your current partners?"

No one said anything so another one of the five friends said, "No, Heather's the problem, like usual."

"Not a problem, Carrie, we want you all to have the best experience you can. If everyone's ready, we'll get started. Heather, come on over here, and I'll introduce you to Bucky. Justin, start here," he pointed at Sadie who was on the end, "and help the others until I get Heather settled."

Mr. Mac led them off in a different direction than

this morning, up sweeping switchbacks and steep ridges this time. Sadie was right behind him and heard his narration of the sights. "The deep rock formations created this valley over a million years ago. Can't you imagine the dinosaurs roaming here and eating giant foliage? We're lucky out here with multiple terrains, places to climb like this, and expansive fields for our horses, cattle, and buffalo to graze. Wild horses used to roam here, too, and we'll talk more about that later."

Sadie admired the pride he had in the land. They got to a flat part of the ridge where they rode side-by-side. Mr. Mac waved Sadie up to come join him at the front. She made sure to stay behind him. She didn't want to get in trouble.

He said, "Now it's your turn. Why don't you tell me something I don't know?"

What would she tell this experienced rancher? Tell him the capital of Maryland is Annapolis? Why would he care?

"Okay, here goes. My dad's in the Navy, and he uses what we call a second language, Navy talk. One of the terms he taught me to use in the horse world is situational awareness."

He repeated, "Situational awareness ... tell me more."

"Kind of like it sounds, paying close attention to what's going on around you. For instance, in a schooling ring and at horse shows, it's not only looking in front of you; it's thinking about how things look. Like if a horse acts like it's about to explode in a fit, or a rider looks like he or she is going to cut someone off, or someone seems nervous."

"Sounds like keeping your wits about you."

Sadie said, "Sort of, and more. Like thinking ahead and noticing small things that may affect others."

"I've never heard that term. I like it, and I'm going to use it."

"Thanks, and I'm glad to help." Sadie was so comfortable with this man who was older than her father. He emanated a warmth and kindness.

"We're about to get to a place I call Loper's Paradise. You'll see why." They rounded a turn into a big, open plain. The sky was even bigger here, which Sadie thought impossible. A hawk circled above, an aerial acrobat, while the white, fluffy clouds traveled in slow motion toward the mountain peaks to the east.

Mr. Mac raised his hand for the group to stop and turned around to address them. Had it only been this morning she learned what that meant?

"Go ahead and spread out. Everybody doing okay?" he asked, looking from one person to the next. "Check your cinches, and if anyone needs help, raise your hand. Justin will help you."

Sadie checked her cinch which was tight, so she unfortunately did not need Justin's help. One of the daughters of the family team raised her hand, and Justin hopped off, leading his horse, to help her. Her name was Juliana, and her mother was Jamie. Juliana was nine, and they traveled from Illinois. She, her sister, Mikayla, and her mother were avid equestrians. But like Sadie, they were neophytes to the ranch life. They called cinches girths and headstalls bridles and were not as sure of the Western saddle parts as they were of their English tack.

"Here we are at Loper's Paradise. We'll take it easy since this is your first lope. Some of your partners have a powerful kickstart, so hold on. Justin will stay behind you all to keep an eye out, but I'm not worried. I watched you all with the eyes in the back of my head. I call it situational awareness." He smiled at Sadie. "Let's go."

They eased into a lope, and the equines moved on cue, out on a plain running as they were built to do. They stretched their legs to meet the ground in the front and caught their back legs up under them to cover that same ground. Not a thundering set of racing hooves, but a graceful, slow, three-beat methodical sound filled the air. Salty tears streamed down Sadie's face from the wind, blurring her vision.

If Sadie should have been scared loping, she didn't know it. She rocked in the deep Western saddle in slow motion. This was nothing like being in a lesson or a horse show with eyes on her at all times. She was free to enjoy the feeling of the horse and breathe the same air sharing a moment of being one entity with a domesticated wild animal. She lived in a dream; Sunny was free to live again.

The group slowed, and Mr. Mac's hand raised at the front. How long had they been loping? She had no idea. Sitting back and gently lifting the reins, Sunny obeyed the command without hesitation. How could someone have tossed this precious mare away? They walked, cooling down.

Sadie sensed a presence next to her, and the thick gray neck of Justin's horse glistened from the lope. She smelled the familiar scent of sweet horse sweat.

"Is he okay? He's lathered up," Sadie said, pointing to the sweat.

"He's fine. Comanche's a big guy and staying behind the others is hard for him. We can't let our horses run off with guests, so we train them not to. It's harder for some than others, like this one here with the huge strides. I like him a lot. All the ranch hands and wranglers train and ride the new ones until they're safe for any rider."

The blowing of the horses' nostrils slowed while Sadie and Justin rode along another green, expansive field. They wound their way around rocks and boulders, and the landscape changed at the bottom of the hill with a sparkling blue river matching the cobalt sky. Cattle grazed about a mile ahead where time stood still.

Mr. Mac led the group to the shore and then waded into the shallow water on a bed of tan, brown, and gray pebbles.

Hooves splashed in the water like children playing in puddles. After a minute, their leader signaled he was stopping. He turned to the group and said, "Go ahead and let them have a drink here. If you brought something in your saddlebags, that goes for you, too."

"How was Sunny?" Justin asked, while Comanche's long neck stretched down slurping the crystal-clear water.

Sadie admired Sunny's graceful neck and listened to her lips playing with the water. Lucky did that, too. "She was perfect, as if she was meant to be here."

"She probably was meant to be. I've never ridden her. Sierra liked her, and the wranglers are above the ranch hands. You know how that goes."

She didn't, but she wasn't going to admit it.

"I'm also tall for her. She looks like she was made for you."

The blood crawled up Sadie's neck, and she was thankful her cowboy hat shaded her face. "Thanks, but she's only mine for a week."

Justin said, "When I first saw her, I thought her name should be Sunny Day. That's what she reminds me of."

"That doesn't sound like a cowboy talking," Sadie joked.

"Not all cowboys are alike."

"Maybe not. Anyhow, I have my own horse back home. His name is Lucky, and he'd fit in nice here, too. I'll show you a picture sometime."

"Thanks, I'd like to see him. I have an idea; why don't you stop by our camp tonight? We're on the compound, not far from the cabins. You can also tell me how you rescued Sunny. Sound good?"

"Okay," Sadie said. "Can I text you if something comes up, and I can't make it?"

"Like what?"

"I don't know." She anticipated her dad wouldn't be supportive of this idea.

"The answer is, we can't have cell phones here. People before us wouldn't stay off their phones when working, so we got stuck with their problem. At least that's what Luke said."

Teenagers without cell phones? It surprised her there wasn't a riot. "I see other people using them all over here, like Sierra, Levi…"

"They're wranglers; we're ranch hands — two different classes of people. We're summer help, and we work for Luke. Wranglers are family, or like family, as Mac said. Most of them have worked here for years."

"Maybe someday," Sadie, the optimist, said.

"Maybe, anyhow, back to the camp, everything will be fine. You'll find it. We find it every day, right?"

"A valid point."

"See you after supper then. I have to go mingle with more guests — all in a day's work." He flashed her a brilliant smile and jogged ahead to Jamie, Juliana, and Mikayla riding together.

What was she thinking? And what would Dad say?

CHAPTER 15

COWBOY CAMP

THE NAVARRO FAMILY FINISHED their second plentiful supper and headed back to the Kalispell cabin for a break before returning for the night's entertainment.

Sadie sidled up to her mom, anxious to share her news. "Mom, that young wrangler, Justin, invited me to their camp tonight. I can't wait!" Sadie said.

"Tell me more about this … camp," Mom said, not looking as excited.

"Oh, Mom, don't be so suspicious. It's where a bunch of the folks who work here live and hang out right here on the property."

Dad piped up; she thought he had been out of earshot. "How old is this Justin, and what do you know about him?"

"He's about my age," Sadie guessed. "He's a hard worker since he works here, and he likes horses."

"That's hardly a background check," Dad challenged.

He didn't understand. He wasn't a girl. Girls know when someone is good or bad. Right?

Mom started, "Jim, she's fourteen. Sadie's bright and mature. I'm sure Mac and Keela wouldn't hire a bunch of criminals to work here." Sadie wanted to hug her mom on the spot.

"Liz — she's fourteen!" Dad said, a bit too loud.

"Right, Dad, and it means I'm a teenager, not a baby anymore. I can't believe you're trying to ruin this for me," Sadie said, looking away.

Austin stepped in and said, "I can go with her." Her brother always had the right answer.

Her parents exchanged looks, and her mother's strong nature showed. There would be further discussion later. Dad appeared defeated.

He said with his usual military precision, "Austin, you will go with Sadie, and stay with her. Take your phone, and if anything seems suspicious, text me *SOS*. You remember what that means, don't you?"

"Yes, Dad, the international distress signal. Remember, I've been living with you my whole life." Austin smiled, defusing the situation more.

"So I can go?" Sadie asked, surprised considering her dad's first reaction.

Grandma spoke for the first time: "Of course you

can go. If Austin hadn't volunteered, I would have gone. Did I tell you about the time…" Grandma looked at Dad and said, "Never mind, another day. As for me, I'm getting ready for tonight. I bought all these clothes for the trip, and I need to wear them while I'm here. Love you, girl!" Grandma kissed Sadie on the cheek and left for her cabin.

"What about me?" Austin asked.

Grandma looked back and blew him a kiss. "Love you, too, Austin."

The Navarros entered their cabin, and Dad turned on the TV, clicking the channels on the remote. Sadie doubted he cared what was on TV. He was trying not to talk. She made herself scarce to freshen up for her date.

Was it a date? No, she was getting carried away with herself. A boy she barely knew had invited her to their camp.

Perhaps they had to do that to be nice to the guests. But she still wanted to at least wash her face, brush her hair, and brush away any corn stuck in her teeth.

When she walked out of the bathroom, Austin asked, "What time is your date?"

"What? What made you say that?"

"One of those things between brothers and sisters. You still haven't answered me."

"He said after supper. You ready?"

He tousled the hair she'd just brushed and said, "I'm ready. No reason for me to get beautiful."

Sadie blushed, and fixed her hair. "Let's go. I wish everyone would stop making this such a big deal."

Austin showed Dad he had his cell phone, and they departed. As soon as they were on the path, Austin said, "Yeah, let's not let it be a big deal. We're a team, remember?"

"Yes, I do, and thanks."

"I need to tell you something while we're alone. I want Mom and Dad to have a decent vacation. They spent a year apart when he was deployed. This is the first time we've been away. This is so different, and I don't want Dad to worry about things."

Her brother sounded so grown up. "The camp shouldn't be far, and it's on the map they gave us." She pointed to the Cowboy Camp on the map. "I brought the map in case we couldn't find it, but Justin said it was easy to find. It says off limits to guests, but we were invited." Actually, she was. Coyotes howled in the wilderness, and Sadie swung her head in that direction. It didn't sound close. If she remembered right, coyotes rarely attacked humans. She hoped she remembered right.

"I'll plug Cowboy Camp into my phone and maybe it will come up on GPS." Austin pulled out his phone pretending to type something in, always the clown.

"Well, he wouldn't have invited me if I couldn't get there by foot. It's probably far enough away so their noise doesn't disturb the guests."

"Sounds like you two had a lot of time to chat." Sadie ignored the comment.

They kept walking on what they thought was the path but didn't find signs of a camp. It was still light enough to see since they were so far north, with no clouds in the sky. Sadie began to wonder if this Justin had sent her on a wild goose chase as some kind of joke. But why would he do that? She smelled smoke.

"That must be the campfire! Let's follow the smell until we see the fire," Sadie said, her mood lightening.

"Whatever you say."

Within minutes, they heard voices, and saw a group of cowboys sitting and standing around a campfire.

When Luke spotted her, Sadie caught a hostile glare in his eyes from across the fire. Sadie had made a mistake and wanted to crawl behind the trees or bushes to disappear.

CHAPTER 16

RANCH HANDS CAMPFIRE

"Um, hi?" she said.

"Sadie! You came!" Justin stood and walked over to join her.

Luke's head swiveled toward Justin with a look of disbelief as he stood. "You invited her?" he asked loudly.

"I didn't think it would be a problem since it's our normal night off. *Is it*?"

Luke answered, "Well … it wouldn't be hospitable of me to ask a guest to leave, would it? And Homeplace Ranch is not that kind of place. Please, come join us. She overheard him mutter to Justin, "I'll deal with you, later."

Sadie stepped forward, and Austin followed. "Howdy," he said sharing an awkward smile.

"What's he doing here?" Justin asked Sadie.

"Do you have a sister?" Austin asked Justin.

"No, but what does that have to do with anything?"

"If you don't have a sister, you wouldn't understand."

Sadie observed the two of them eyeing each other up like two horses in a new herd, trying to decide who would be more dominant. Justin submitted.

"What do you guys do out here anyway?" Austin asked.

"We're not all guys," a feminine voice spoke from the opposite side of the flames. She rose from the log she sat on and tipped her hat. "Kitty's the name, and to answer your question, we—"

A male ranch hand said, "The answer is, none of your business. He invited the girl, not you."

"Cash, don't be rude," Luke said. "This big brother here is doing his job. I'm guessing the parents didn't want their little girl out here all alone with a bunch of rough and tumble cowboys." Sadie winced.

Austin spoke with confidence, "All I see so far is talking."

Kitty's straight strawberry-blonde hair swung with her as she shook her head and laughed. Even in a cowboy hat, jean jacket, and no makeup, she could pass for a supermodel.

Sadie remembered Mr. Mac introducing her and had seen her helping guests. Now she was close enough to see how striking she was. Envy slithered in.

"Since we have unexpected company, let's do something different tonight," Luke said.

Eyes darted from person to person. Sadie got an uneasy feeling, or was it an unsafe one?

Then he said, "Let's play some music!"

"Yeah! Been a while," Cash said. "You all will get to hear me sing again!" The crew groaned.

"Take a seat by the fire, guests," Luke said, "and we'll be right back. I think you've met everyone except Doug and Carlos." He pointed to each when he said their names. "Don't try talking to Carlos because he doesn't speak much English."

Sadie said to Carlos in Spanish, "I speak Spanish."

Carlos nodded, and replied to her in Spanish, which Luke didn't understand. "I speak more English than he thinks. I'm quiet — something he doesn't understand." Sadie laughed.

Luke said, "Don't do that."

Sadie hesitated. "Why? I'm trying to be friendly."

Luke tightened his lips. "Because he needs to learn English, and that doesn't help. I'm sure you understand." She didn't.

Luke left, and the ranch hands followed him. Sadie told herself he was planning to put together a cowboy symphony or something to entertain them. Loud Luke certainly had some quirks.

Austin pulled out his phone acting like he was ready to send a text, and said, "The code's *SOS*, right?" He chuckled and gave her a soft punch on her bicep. "Lighten up, sis. You worry too much." He was right.

The ensemble returned after a while, one at a time, with instruments — a guitar, a small drum, a cowbell, a harmonica, and some type of wind instrument.

Justin sat on the log next to Sadie. Kitty pointed to the seat next to Austin and asked, "Anyone here?" He shook his head, one of the few times Sadie had seen him speechless. She flashed him a welcoming smile and took her place next to him. Everyone else got situated, and Luke strummed the guitar playing a country tune Sadie recognized.

"When is he going to start singing?" Austin asked Kitty.

"He won't; he plays but doesn't sing. You sure ask a lot of questions." She looked him in the eye. In the firelight, Sadie saw she had large hazel eyes with what resembled a yellow sunflower planted in the middle surrounded by a prism of blue, green, and brown rays. She was naturally beautiful.

"This is all new to me. Yesterday morning my sister and I were in Maryland, and today we're out in the middle of nowhere with a bunch of strangers. I want to understand everything."

"Why don't you experience it instead? You don't have to understand," Kitty said.

"But I want to. I want to understand how you all live, and like, do you have any family?"

"That's another world; this is this world. This is what I want — horses, country, and a family, even if we are a dysfunctional family out here." She laughed. "This group here, we're not the ranch family over there. We're our own family." She fidgeted with a guitar pick in her hands.

She glanced at him and said, "I'm trying to make a life on my own."

Sadie heard that and thought, "On her own?" Kitty couldn't be that much older than she was. Although Sadie didn't see herself as a kid anymore, she wasn't ready to pay rent, buy food, and do whatever else came with being on her own.

"Miss Kitty!" a voice across the fire summoned. "Your turn!"

"Miss Kitty?" Austin asked.

"There you go with more questions! The guys call me that, from some old TV show. The older guests seem to like it. I don't mind. Sounds ladylike, don't you think?"

"I think they're all waiting for you and staring at me, and I don't think they like me much anyhow. If you like the name, I do, too," Austin said.

The poised girl strolled across the campfire like a rock

star taking the stage while the others clapped politely for Luke's performance. "May I?" Kitty asked Luke, reaching for the guitar.

"It's yours, isn't it?" Luke smirked at her.

Sadie noticed the mood at the camp lifted with the music. Kitty studied the guitar strings intensely. She tuned strings, strummed a few chords, and followed with a thump on the guitar.

"This one is an original, and I'll dedicate it to our new friends from Maryland. Welcome to our little slice of Montana!"

The chatter stopped, and her low, soulful alto voice filled the air. Kitty sang of love lost, and emptiness, and it was as if she were bearing her soul in words and music.

"I just want to be loved,

Looking for a home for my heart.

Not asking for much, just want to be loved,

A wanderer looking for my start."

Kitty continued, and Sadie watched as everyone became mesmerized while listening to many verses. When the song came to its end, the ranch hand, Doug, applauded, and others followed.

Sadie asked, "You wrote that song?"

"Yeah, I mean, I'm still working on it and everything."

"Why? It's amazing," Austin said.

"Come on, Miss Kitty, give us another one," one of the ranch hands said. "And sing a happy one, will ya?"

Kitty looked away, appearing relieved to be out of the conversation with Austin and Sadie. "Okay, but I need company. There's plenty of instruments, and the rest of you can bang on a rock or something. Get creative!"

Kitty played an upbeat tune everyone knew, an oldie but goodie, John Denver's "Thank God I'm a Country Boy." Carlos beat the drum, and Doug blew random notes into the harmonica. Cash chimed in with the wind instrument. Was it a Native American version of a recorder? Luke banged a cowbell which was a real live recycled cowbell, not one made to be an instrument.

Justin asked Sadie, "Having fun?"

"Yes! I never did anything like this. Do you do this often?"

"Nah, we did it a night or two when we first started, but not much now. Most nights, we—"

"Hey, you two should be singing along and banging rocks or something," Luke hollered from his seat.

"What do you do most nights?" Sadie asked, always inquisitive.

"Work, chores, cleaning tack, that kind of stuff."

Luke showed up next to Sadie, handing her the cowbell. She tapped the stick on it as if she played it every day, trying to make the bees buzzing in her stomach go away. Those bees hadn't visited since horse shows. Concentrating on the beat, she banged in rhythm until the song ended, pleased with her contribution to the concert.

"Anyone else?" Kitty asked the others. "Talent, anyone?"

They shook their heads and laughed. Kitty stood up and brought the guitar to Justin.

"And for our last act, our own Justin Johnson, whose next stop will be Nashville, Tennessee!"

"No thanks, Miss Kitty. I think you're doing a fine job."

"Too bad, your turn. You don't want to hear Cash again, do you?" She turned around and didn't look back, finding her place next to Austin.

Sadie wondered how all these people knew how to play the guitar. She had tried instruments with no success. She liked listening to music but wasn't wired to play. Well, except for the cowbell. Hey, she found her talent in case she had to perform.

Justin sang his version of the first non-country tune of the night. He played Bruno Mars' "Just the Way You Are." During the refrain, the guys had fun with the high notes, and Kitty joined in to help them with the tough ones. She could sing for sure and had an amazing range. The background chorus included "da-das" and "ba-bas," which the outsiders joined in on. Justin stared straight at her at one point, and the pang she felt reminded her of the way she and Lucky connected. The singer didn't miss a beat in his song. She was overreacting.

She told herself to stop. She didn't even know this guy. This better not become a trend in her life because she didn't like her emotions being out of control. Lost in her thoughts, Justin finished his song to applause.

"Let's wrap it up, folks," Luke said. "We've had enough fun for one night. Don't get used to it. Back to work tomorrow."

Sadie didn't want to leave.

Justin said to her, "Thank you for coming. I'm glad you'll be here until Saturday."

"Thank you — this has been the most fun here, well, besides the horses. Oh, and wait," she pulled out her phone. "I came here to show you a picture of Lucky, and here he is."

"Wow, thanks, that's some horse. I hope you can come back again and tell me Sunny's story." Justin put his right hand to his heart and tapped his chest twice.

She wasn't sure what he meant, but it gave her a strange tingling sensation. She got back to the conversation at hand. "Coming back doesn't seem like a good idea. I'm sorry your boss is mad at you."

"He'll get over it. People do."

Austin walked up and said, "Time to go, sis. Not my rules, but the boss's." He pointed backward to Luke and relayed a comical disapproving look from Luke she understood.

"You're right. We shouldn't overstay our welcome."

"I think we did that when we showed up," her brother said.

"Bye, Justin." Sadie waved and felt like a kid. He waved back.

Sadie departed on a cloud, until that voice traveled the distance when Luke likely thought they were out of range.

"Don't you ever do that again, boy. You wanna be a cowboy? If so, you need to think and act like a cowboy, not like a love-struck kid."

Sadie hoped she heard wrong and hoped Austin hadn't heard at all.

CHAPTER 17

WESTERN CLINIC

SADIE RODE WESTERN WHEN she lived out in California but not so much since moving to Maryland. Loftmar Stables focused on hunter and jumper disciplines, which Sadie quickly adjusted to. She still liked Western and looked forward to the clinic she signed up for to brush up on her skills. Yesterday it was a better idea before she got to know Justin. Now she was here for the day instead of being out on the trails but would make the best of it.

Mr. Mac led the clinic in a sand arena behind the red barn. Speaking to the assembled group, he said, "We train and practice natural horsemanship techniques here at the ranch. It takes longer, but we have time. We don't believe in harsh methods akin to animal cruelty. We believe in helping riders learn to communicate with their horses. Improved communication leads to a trust and respect between riders and their equine partners."

Sierra assisted her father today, and Carlos was on hand, too. They paired everyone up with their horses for the day, and all listened to instructions while mounted. Pamela's wide smile glowed while she massaged Tanner's withers; clearly, she had bonded with him.

Mr. Mac rode Reckless, one of the mustangs he had rescued from a Bureau of Land Management (BLM) auction. Mac explained, "Some of you may think she has an odd name for being as mild-mannered as she is, not reckless at all. We named her after the brave mare Sergeant Reckless who fought with the U.S. Marines in the Korean War. It's a name of honor for this girl with lots of heart." A newcomer to the herd, Reckless would be continuing her training and learning along with everyone else today.

Homeplace paired Sadie with Tabasco, a ranch veteran who knew what to do in a Western clinic. Sierra explained that Sunny wasn't ready for the clinic because it included events she hadn't been trained in yet. Although disappointed, Sadie understood and admitted she already liked her tall sorrel Thoroughbred with a wide white blaze and two hind matching socks. She hadn't imagined riding a Thoroughbred at a ranch but knew of the breed's versatility.

After explaining the schedule, Sierra asked, "Can you all please introduce yourselves and describe your riding experience?" After listening, Sadie was happy to not be the only Western rider with not much serious Western experience. The students included Pamela and her parents; two people from the Bad Guys group — Eddy and the three-timer, Debbie — and Sadie.

Mr. Mac, the horseman, sported a giant silver belt buckle, denim shirt, and khaki cowboy hat today. He finished up the introductory remarks: "I think you'll find if you listen, learn from your horses, and watch each other, you'll have a good day. Let's warm up."

He instructed the riders to begin walking in a serpentine pattern starting at one side of the ring going toward the other. Cones formed the snake pattern, and he encouraged them to look ahead, not down, and to keep their shoulders square making their turns.

"Feel your horse, find the back, follow the shoulder. Don't sit there like a sack of potatoes — move with him or her. Help your horse walk, turn, and feel the dance with you. Remember, this is a partnership. If you're not looking for a partnership, change your sport, and go buy a bicycle. You want your horse to want to be with you. You should want to be with your partner. The way to make that bond is to make it comfortable for both of you."

Sadie listened to Mr. Mac's words and transported

herself to a different world, concentrating on how simple it sounded. She thought back to her earliest riding days and remembered the singular enjoyment of being on a horse. She used to imagine being a girl centaur, as if the horse and she were one. Today she felt that way.

"Breathe in, breathe out," continued the soothing voice. "See if you can match your breathing to your horse's movements. People underestimate the power of breath, but let's concentrate and see how your breathing affects your ride. It's part of the communication."

Once Sadie let her body move with the horse and thought about her breathing, her actions connected with her horse. She pursed her lips and pushed the air out hard deepening her seat bones in the saddle signaling Tabasco to "whoa." She learned this before, but it became clearer having it as her only focus. Tabasco understood, too.

Sierra said, "Remember, we may be the human leaders, but we have to listen to our partners. Or else, we can't win as a team."

The clinic continued with slow, methodical exercises designed to help riders communicate with their horses. The rider/horse combination connections varied, some better than others. Sadie enjoyed the pole bending exercise where Tabasco negotiated the course and snaked in and out of the poles without touching them. He seemed to like the challenge, and she liked the feeling of following his lean, muscled body through the pattern. She focused on her breathing, made sure not to ride too forceful or too passive, and praised her horse partner. Most of all, she remembered to have fun.

Sierra and Mr. Mac helped the riders learn the pattern they would perform at the end of the day for the final event — the competition. Homeplace talked so much about horsemanship and the connection between horse and rider, and Sadie wondered how they would judge that. It came naturally to her, no matter the horse. This wouldn't change between now and the competition anyway, so she was happy she and Tabasco had already created a relationship. She had one less thing to worry about.

They broke for lunch, giving both horses and humans a break. Keela and Morgan delivered a feast of sliced sandwiches, fried chicken, chips, and fresh-baked chocolate chip cookies. Sadie lined up next to Carlos, the ranch hand she'd met last night. She didn't say much to him this morning, busy with the clinic. She decided to be friendly again. He must be lonely out here with no one to talk to.

Practicing her rusty Spanish, she said, "Hi again. You know if you need someone to talk to, or directions translated, or whatever, I can try. As you can tell, my Spanish isn't the best, but I know the basics."

"*Gracias,*" he said, looking skittish.

"I have an Uncle Carlos, although he's a lot older than us. Do you want to have lunch together? I'd like to practice my Spanish, and maybe Pamela will join us."

"It would be nice to talk to someone who understands me." He laughed. They sat at one of the nearby picnic tables probably there for this exact reason.

Digging into the best fried chicken ever, she waited for Carlos to start the conversation. Wow, he said he was quiet, and he meant it. She gave it a shot. "Who is your favorite horse here?"

"All of them. I don't like the mules as much; they're not the same. But Mr. Mac, he gets good horses. I like helping train them. My family always said I had a way with them, so I decided to put it to use."

Now he was talking! "My favorite, of course, is Sunny. However, I'm enjoying Tabasco today. They are all so different, like people."

He nodded. "Sunny … did you know palomino is a Spanish word?"

"No, I didn't. Never thought about it."

"Aha! So I can tell you something then." He seemed pleased. "It means *young dove* based on the horse's coloring. For Sunny, it's right, because she's so calm."

"Funny, because when I found out she was coming out here, I was a wreck. But in meeting her and riding her, she's made it all better, like peaceful. I'm getting all weird on you. You probably wish I didn't speak Spanish!"

"Don't say that. I've enjoyed it. But don't do it in front of Luke." He avoided her eyes.

"Sadie!" Pamela arrived, following lunch with her parents. "And Carlos, *mucho gusto*." She said, telling him in Spanish it was a pleasure to meet him. Sadie remembered her European friends regularly spoke several languages. And here Sadie was stammering out her weak Spanish.

The three chatted about horses, homes, the clinic, and food. Before long, Sierra politely let each table know they were getting ready to start part two of the clinic. The three of them finished up and made their way back to the action.

Once remounted, Mr. Mac called everyone into a circle and explained the rules for the competition. "You will be judged on a series of four events, and they will be the following: 1) barrels, 2) poles, 3) walk, jog, lope, and 4) Western riding pattern. We've learned and practiced all the things you need to succeed with these today. We'll do one event at a time, like a rodeo."

Sadie patted Tabasco's neck, closed her eyes, and whispered, "I believe," a ritual she shared with horses since Austin first discovered those special words spelled out in Lucky's markings. For the first two events, she took a deep breath and remembered which direction to go. Tabasco knew what to do, and Sadie paid attention to what she had learned this morning. When she calmly let her horse glide her through the poles without interfering, her fellow students hooted and howled. They crossed the finish line, but not in the fastest time so far. They'd done their best, which was good enough for her.

The walk, jog, lope event proved easy for Sadie. She practiced this in walk, trot, canter competitions in Maryland which was way more stressful than this. Her partner was a breeze to ride, unlike her younger and less trained, or greener, Lucky. In her eyes, the Western pattern would challenge her the most of the four events because the rider must remember the prescribed pattern in his or her head. Unlike barrels or pole bending, the horse won't do it from memory because the patterns change all the time. A rider can lose with one wrong move.

Mr. Mac must have sensed Sadie's apprehension before the pattern competition began. He approached her on foot before Sierra called her turn.

"Point your eyes where you want to go, and he'll follow you. Don't worry about it. You know this pattern." He touched his fist to her knee and smiled before he walked away. He believed in her. She couldn't let him down.

Having gone first and feeling good about her ride, she watched and cheered on the rest of the riders wondering where she stood. She was a rookie compared to some, and more experienced than others. But she had an advantage. She got the horse and rider connection, and she appreciated her Tabasco. Every horse had its own personality, and it's up to the human to figure it out.

After everyone went and what seemed like an eternity, Mr. Mac announced, "We have the results of the competition! Remember, horsemanship is our key evaluation factor. Our winner is Sadie. And our reserve champion is Debbie. Congratulations to everyone on your hard day's work and to your horses for their work for you today. I hope you learned something and had a good time."

She would use the training all week and when she got home, with fond memories of her cowgirl up clinic day.

~

CHAPTER 18

A WAY OF LIFE

FOR TONIGHT'S ENTERTAINMENT, SADIE boarded the touring bus with the other guests to attend the town rodeo. Although a functional people mover, the vehicle seemed out of place at the ranch. She looked forward to seeing a real Montana town and a live rodeo. She watched professional bull riding on TV and rodeo scenes in movies, but today's clinic was her closest to any real rodeo action.

Mom and Dad took two seats, and Sadie and Austin sat behind them. People filed in shuffling for seats and talking among themselves; it was anything but quiet. Grandma found her Canadian girl group and sat with them. She had an outfit for every event, and tonight's rodeo attire included a red suede jacket with fringes and matching red boots. She wore a black cow hair belt with silver rhinestone designs of longhorn steer heads.

Tiny in frame and stature, Grandma was adorable in her cowgirl duds.

When Tony and Regina started down the bus aisle, they waved at Mom and Dad. Regina pointed at the two seats across from them, smiling and nodding. Dad reached over and patted the seat welcoming them. The parents joined the parents there, and Pamela sat across the aisle from Sadie and Austin.

Austin stood up. "Here, you two can sit together."

Pamela put her hand over her heart. "Are you sure?"

"Yes, I can talk to her anytime. Go ahead, please." Austin eyed the people standing behind her waiting to pass.

Pamela took the seat next to Sadie and said to Austin, "Who will sit with you?"

"Don't worry about him," Sadie said. "He's like my dad; he makes friends with everyone."

"A nice quality, no?" Pamela asked.

"I suppose," Sadie answered.

A blonde woman, Leah, pointed to the seat next to Austin and asked, "Seat taken?"

"Only if you want it," Austin said smiling. He stood and let her in. As soon as she settled in, he turned to her making conversation. By the time they got to the rodeo, her brother would know everything about her. He had a way of doing that.

Sierra and Blake walked down the aisle counting heads, one counting each side until they got to the back. Mr. Mac boarded the bus last and asked them, "We all here?" They must have answered yes because the trip moved to the next phase.

Mr. Mac clipped on a microphone and continued facing the passengers while standing. "Let's get this show on the road." The driver engaged the gears and pulled away. "Cowboys and cowgirls, you're in for a treat. We're a small town with one of the best rodeos in the country. Lots of rodeos only run on the weekends, but the Settlers Rodeo holds a rodeo on Tuesdays during the summer. They do this to support our local ranches and give the competitors more time to practice and make, or take, extra bucks." He threw his head down and up like a horse making a buck.

Laughs rippled through the bus.

"The sport of rodeo originated from the old American West working lifestyle, and it's become big business. The National Finals Rodeo awards more than ten million dollars in prize money these days, and the local rodeos leading up to the king of all rodeos award decent prizes. But to us, it's not about the money.

"Rodeo is a way to preserve our history, our culture, and our way of life. It's about family; you'll see. It helps teach kids to dream, to work hard, to compete, and to take care of their animals. Well, I'll shut up and sit down and let you all do whatever you were doing. I'll talk to you again when we're five minutes out." He sat in the front seat behind the driver and pulled out his cell phone. Mr. Mac was one busy man.

"Your cowboy is here in the back," Pamela said. Sadie hadn't seen Justin on the bus.

"Where?"

"In the back, silly; he walked right by you counting heads."

"He's not my cowboy. I told you, he's all yours," Sadie said.

"Then who were you looking for?" Pamela flashed a slight smile, and her eyes lit up.

"No one." She was uncomfortable with that lie, and her friend wouldn't take her eyes off of her.

Sadie whispered, "I thought Justin would be here. He's been nice to me."

"Why such a secret?" Pamela also whispered.

"I don't know; he's a friend and nothing more. Hard to explain, but it seems like there's something different about him. New subject, do you have a boyfriend?"

Pamela waved her hand in the air and said, "Many, but no cowboys," and winked at her. Sadie loved how dramatic she was; she could be an actress. "Yet," she finished.

"Tonight could be the night," Sadie said.

Pamela looked to the back of the bus where Blake stood, speaking to a lady guest with one hand on the top of her headrest. "I'd better move fast."

"You're too funny. You know, my home state has a Maryland High School Rodeo, and kids compete from all across the state. I never paid much attention to it, but it's something I'll look into when I'm home. I mean, today was great, and I've ridden Lucky Western. He can do it; he can do anything."

"Yes! And with his flashy colors, you'll win all the prizes. I'm so jealous," Pamela said.

The two continued their conversation, and the noise level rose with lively discussions in all directions. Before they knew it, Mr. Mac was standing in his spot again and speaking into the microphone.

"Hello out there!" The voices trailed off. "Thank you. I wanted to mention a few more things. First, you'll see food and drink concession stands on the grounds and booths selling crafts, souvenirs, and trinkets. I ask that everyone follow me to our seats first and go back shopping later if you'd like, or else we may never get to our seats.

"One last thing to do before we arrive. From what I heard on the way here, this task won't be a hard one for this crowd." He smiled ear to ear. "We're going to practice making noise."

"You see, every Tuesday, the local ranches bring their

guests to this rodeo. The announcer will ask each of the groups to make a shout-out of where they are sitting as a greeting. Homeplace always wins. We don't want to break that record, do we?"

Shouts of "no" and "boo" erupted.

"So let's hear it. On the count of three — one, two, and three." He pointed at the crowd, and a chorus of yip yips, yahoos, clapping, and whistling filled the bus.

He cleared his throat and shook his head. "Okay, let's try that again, if Oak Springs Ranch beats us, I'll never hear the end of it. Here we go again — on one, two, and *three*."

The decibel level rose again, and Mr. Mac motioned his hands upward encouraging the group to holler, clap, and whistle louder. When it reached a certain level, he nodded and smiled, and motioned his hands back down.

"That will do. I didn't think y'all would let me and the Homeplace crew down. We'll be there in a minute. When we stop, follow me to the best seats in the house."

The rodeo arena was bigger than Sadie had imagined with bleacher seats rising to meet the bright lights at the top to highlight the action. Country music blared, contributing to the festive mood. Spectators milled about and found their seats. Families sat together ranging from toddlers to grandparents. This was a small town with a large heart.

The group followed Mr. Mac to their section chatting among themselves. Austin introduced Sadie and his parents to his bus companion, Leah Mulhall. It turned out Leah had been in the Army, had served in Afghanistan like Dad, and came on this trip as a reward to herself for ending her service. Dad latched on to the military connection and invited her to sit with them. Leah said yes, and Sadie surmised she and Dad would talk military stuff all night. Whatever made them happy.

Blake met up with Sadie, and said, "Welcome to Utica. Most people are surprised by the size of our rodeo."

"I would agree with them. I didn't know what to expect, but not this." She turned to Pamela, "What do you think?"

"I love it. It reminds me of festivals in my country, American style. So, Mr. Blake, do you rodeo?"

"Please, I'm Blake, not much older than you. My dad is the *mister* here. The answer is 'no.' I used to. But with the family business, there's not much spare time. I can't complain; I get more than my fair share of time in the saddle."

"Would you mind sitting with us? I mean, I don't know anything about rodeo. Could you help explain, please?" Pamela asked.

Yep, her friend was good at this.

"Mighty kind of you, Pamela, I think I will. Save me

a seat, and as soon as Dad, Sierra, and I have everyone set, I'll be over. *Ciao,*" Blake said, as he moved on to the next group. He was equally good at this.

Great. Sadie had been able to avoid him as much as possible, and he'd be with them all night. She tried to do her friend a favor, and it backfired. How bad could it be? She would make sure he sat on the far side of Pamela away from her. Nothing would ruin Sadie's first rodeo.

CHAPTER 19

➳

THE SETTLERS
RODEO

THE HOMEPLACE GANG SAT together, and the event began right on time. The announcer's booming voice welcomed them to the Settlers Rodeo and gave a brief history and overview of what was to come. Rodeo clowns entertained, performing antics for different sections of the crowd. A ladies' precision drill team dressed in glittery cowgirl costumes performed flawless maneuvers and waved American flags. Enthusiasm radiated from both the performers and the spectators.

"It's time for our national anthem. Please rise and remove your hats. Remain standing for the Cowboy's Prayer." Sadie sneaked a peek at her dad as they sang "The Star-Spangled Banner." Neither of them could make it through the full song without tearing up. She smiled and wiped her tear with the back of her hand. What was wrong with being a proud American?

Blake told Pamela, "We're patriotic here in Montana. Our state law requires a flag in every classroom. It's part of our way of life."

"I like that," Pamela answered. "We Italians are proud of our country, too." Sadie wanted to congratulate her friend for her subtle way of letting him know she had something to say as well.

Next, the announcer welcomed each of the ranch groups asking which could cheer the loudest. The others must not have practiced, or they didn't have as many competitive characters, because Homeplace won hands down. With the opening ceremonies over, it was time to get on with the show.

"Our first event will be bareback riding, sure to be action-packed, and first up is Trevor Montgomery. Let's cheer on Trevor riding Lightning Pete!"

The rider exploded out of the chute holding onto an apparatus made of leather and something unidentifiable. Lightning Pete moved fast and bucked hard in every direction. Sadie had no idea how he held on with one hand. Her body tensed, hoping he didn't fall, and then the high-pitched horn wailed. The scoreboard showed he lasted the necessary eight seconds. The rider dismounted to a buck and got right to his feet, while another rider, a pickup man, got hold of the stray horse.

He must have ridden well because he stayed on, and from the cheers, he had a decent score. From what Sadie could tell, his legs moved rhythmically, but he sat so far back in an awkward position as if lying down at times. She didn't want to ask Blake anything so was happy Pamela asked him.

"How do they score this? Other than the time?"

Blake explained, like he probably had one hundred times to clueless guests: "It's a combination of things. The rider's control, the way they spur, and how the horse performs. Half the points are for the rider, and half the points are for the horse. The riders don't pick that horse; they randomly draw, you know the expression, the old luck of the draw."

"What makes them buck like that?" Pamela asked. "It seems so … unnatural."

He leaned in. "They breed horses and bulls for this sport. They know it's their job. Next time look for the flank strap, which people think makes them buck. But it doesn't. The strap makes them kick out instead of rearing and makes the bucking action stronger. They say the seasoned horses and bulls associate the strap with show time."

He seemed to like being an entertainer like his dad. Sadie had to ask him, "Doesn't it hurt?"

"No, and that's another thing people think. It's more like wearing a tight belt. It isn't meant to hurt the animals, because if it did, they wouldn't perform."

With each rider, they learned more, either from the announcer or Blake. Who knew there were so many rules in rodeo? Riders got disqualified if they touched themselves, their horses, or their equipment with the free hand they swung around to stay balanced. And, of course, their ride ended with no score if they landed on the ground before the eight seconds.

Blake and Pamela hit it off well, and Pamela glowed. She found her cowboy, even if only for a few hours at a rodeo. Sadie felt like a third wheel on their date. Next up came events that didn't interest her: steer wrestling and team roping. The poor steer looked so confused, although the horses looked like they liked their jobs.

Sadie said, "I'm going to go find a drink. Anybody want anything?"

"I'll take a water if you don't mind?" Pamela answered, and Blake shook his head.

"You want me to tell you where the concessions are?" Blake asked.

"No thanks, I saw them on the way in. I want to check things out and pick up a trinket or two. See you soon." She left out the fact she was going to search for Justin thinking he might be there. As the only event in town for the night, he must have made his way to it. Sadie looked toward her dad and gestured she was going to get a drink. He caught her eye briefly and nodded, seeming to be engrossed in the conversation with his new military friend Leah and the action in the arena.

The grounds were carnival-like with horses and live-stock instead of rides. Popcorn and cotton candy smells filled the air; colorful lights decorated the grounds; and people dressed in true cowboy and cowgirl gear mingled about whether working or enjoying their night out.

She scanned the faces looking for any familiar ranch hands and came across a series of booths selling local wares. Wanting something unique, she skipped over the T-shirt and clothing stands. A Native American woman behind a table worked on creating an intricate dream-catcher with feathers, strings, and beads. Hand-crafted ornaments, jewelry, wind chimes, and artwork hung from tree branch displays arranged symmetrically on her table.

"Can I help you find something?" she asked.

"No thank you," Sadie said, and then changed her mind. "I'm looking for a special gift for a friend."

She nodded and placed the dreamcatcher behind her to give Sadie her undivided attention. "What kind of friend?"

"He's my neighbor, and he's helping me out by taking care of my horse while I'm out here on vacation." Why was she babbling?

The woman reached under the table covered with a decorative woven blanket. She rummaged around, pulled out a felt pouch, and handed it to Sadie. Her eyes gleaming, she said, "I think this may be perfect."

Opening the odd-sized pouch, Sadie was unsure what she would find. She pulled out a unique hoof pick with a light tan wooden handle decorated with a dark brown arrow design. On the end, a small leather loop attached to a fastener so it could be hung from a belt loop or a hook in a barn. "It's beautiful. How did you know?"

The storekeeper appeared pleased. "I could tell by your voice it had to be unique. My son made this."

"You were right; it's perfect. I'll take it; I won't find anything better than this."

She paid for it and thanked her. As Sadie departed, the woman said, "I'm glad it's going to the right home!" What an interesting choice of words considering why Sadie was here.

Elated with her purchase, she tied the small pouch to her belt loop, so she wouldn't misplace it in her travels. She surveyed the crowd and her surroundings and recognized a face she didn't want to see standing in front of a barn — Luke. Since he was there, it made sense the others would be, too. They hadn't been on the bus, but neither had he.

Sadie didn't want to ask Luke about Justin because he obviously didn't like her. Instead, she scouted out a way to get near the barn where the rest of the crew would probably be found. The ranch hands had all been nice enough to her; Luke was the problem. Winding around a circuitous route to keep herself out of sight, she found a way to check out the barn. She crept around the back of it and found it quiet except for horses gnawing hay and an occasional snort.

She couldn't help but hear the conversation in front of the barn.

"I hated to come all the way here to chase you down. People are getting anxious the way you skipped town so fast," said a man who must have been the one she saw Luke with in front of the barn. He was loud like Luke. It must be a rodeo thing.

"I didn't skip town. I got a job at a ranch here. Can't rodeo without my roping horse, and I can't do the rough stock riding anymore."

"I know all about your horse, and I was there for the accident. I sat with you in the hospital because your old man refused to visit."

Luke said, "I remember. But you didn't come here to talk about that, did you?"

The older man softened his tone: "So you got a job at one of those dude ranches? You hit rock bottom, buddy. Catering to all those spoiled brats and city folk. I can't imagine."

"I can only go up from here." Luke forced a chuckle that didn't quite sound right.

"I'm worried about you, boy. People want the money you owe them. Those boys are always looking for a fight, and I wouldn't put it past them to rough you up bad."

Sadie sucked in air. Did they hear that?

"I have a plan, Butch. But the plan is taking time."

"You had time. You're out of time. I'm here to pass on a message, a warning you need to listen to. You have two weeks to come up with another payment, or else." It was clear to Sadie at a distance, what "or else" meant.

"You know I'm good for my word. I'm not perfect, but I'm not a thief."

"I've known you since you were a kid, living with the meanest old man around. Lately you made some dumb decisions. I told you not to buy that horse. You couldn't afford him, and it was too risky."

"Did you come here to tell me I'm stupid because my dad's not around to do that anymore?" Luke asked.

"No, I'm coming to warn you. I can't afford to bail you out of this one. And to talk some sense into you so you don't do something this stupid again. I told you to watch out for those Zena's Skip offspring; they're prone to suspensory issues, especially when you start 'em too early. I told you if you saw something early to slow down, back off, and give him time. They're topnotch animals, but they take time to mature," Butch continued.

"I know, and instead I pushed him to win. Because of that, he's gone. I regret that and feel terrible about it. He was my horse, and my best shot at making it big. But I can't do much about that except for finding a way to pay the bill. I figured that out."

"And then that girl left."

"Let's not go there," he said. Was that hurt in his voice?

Butch paused. "You still got her horse. Why don't you sell that mare? She's a winner — would bring in top dollar."

"Because she's not mine to sell! I told you I'm not a thief, and definitely not a horse thief. I have a plan for her to make money doing barrels, but it's taking time."

"They said you got two weeks. I didn't tell them where you are, but it wouldn't be hard to figure out. I'm your friend. They are not your friends. Time for me to take that long trip back. Take care, son, and I am sorry about your horse ... and the girl."

"I'm sorry, too. I need to get back to the ranch." Luke's voice cracked. "Butch, thanks for coming. You shouldn't have to come clean up my messes."

"You're right, but I owe it to your old man." The stranger's boots crunched in the dirt floor moving away from the barn.

Shaken, Sadie turned to retreat the way she entered. Not watching where she was going, the metal bucket turned over with a clang. She ducked into the closest empty stall and crouched down out of sight.

Slow footsteps entered the aisle way, likely investigating the source of the noise. It had to be Luke; no one else was around. The steps stopped outside her hiding place, close enough for Sadie to smell a nasty mix of dried sweat and tobacco. Holding her breath, she remained still. He took a few more steps, righted the bucket with a bang and mumbled, "Cats, rats, figures." Seemingly satisfied with his discovery, he departed.

Rats? That was close. Exhaling, she counted, *one, two, three,* counting to thirty to make sure he left while listening for scurrying rat sounds. Her mind raced. She needed to get back. How long had she been gone, and would they notice?

Heading toward the arena, she had enough wits about her to stop for the drinks she had left for. Sadie arrived at her seat, and Pamela said, "We thought we lost you!" She tilted her head. "Are you okay?"

"I'm fine, thanks." Was she?

"Too much excitement here at the rodeo," Pamela patted her thigh.

True, but Pamela didn't know why. "Anything exciting happen here?"

Pamela answered, "Lots! You missed some events, but here comes the last of the saddle bronc riders. I'm glad we didn't have to do this at the clinic today!"

Sadie watched, her mind far away, back to the conversation she shouldn't have heard. He hurt a horse. She knew how bad it felt to have a hurt horse. But it sounded like it was his fault. He lost a girl. Because of the horse? And he owed people money.

She didn't like him after last night, and now she liked him less. She sat silent through the tie-down roping, and perked up at the cowgirl sport, barrel racing. Was it only this afternoon she practiced her own hand at this?

"Look, this is what you and Lucky will do if you join that rodeo in Maryland!" Pamela chattered.

The entire arena came alive with the fast-paced barrel racing. The crowds gasped when barrels tipped, putting those riders out of competition due to the five-second penalty. Sadie wondered about Luke's reference to the barrel horse. And what had happened to the girl they talked about?

Before she knew it, bull riding started. Those enormous beasts with names like Maximus Kick tried their best to unseat their riders. It scared her how close the bull's horns came to human flesh at times. She learned the importance of rodeo clowns, also called bull fighters, who distracted bulls and protected riders once they dismounted, either on their own or not.

The rodeo ended, and plenty had happened in two hours. The sport of rodeo became less of a mystery to her. But another situation presented a new mystery involving Homeplace Ranch and its lead ranch hand.

CHAPTER 20

HUMMINGBIRDS

SADIE ENJOYED THE WAY Levi shared his life in the saddle stories with the guests during rides. A tour guide, safety chief, and horseman extraordinaire, Sadie would not forget him. He stopped at a plateau at the end of a long climb. To Sadie's surprise, a fenced corral sat off to the left in the grass. Rocks formed thousands of years ago decorated the right side of the landscape. Skinny paths carved their way through the trees creating shady knolls.

When the riders made their way to the spot, they formed a semicircle around their guide. Levi said, "This is our lunch spot today. We will help you with your horses who also get to take a break and have a grass snack." He pointed to the corral. "Pull those lunches Keela made this morning out of your saddlebags. Find yourselves a comfy spot in one of the cubbyholes nature made for you."

"How long is the break?" Austin asked. Sadie smiled

at her time-conscious brother. If Dad had been here, he would have asked the same thing before Austin did. Time didn't cross Sadie's mind at all.

"We'll be here for an hour, so take your time. Walk around, stretch your legs, head out on that trail between the two tall rock formations over there and treat yourself to one of our fresh springs. But don't get lost! We have stories to tell at the Miner's Hollow campfire at night about guests who wandered too far."

Laughs arose from among the group, and Levi dismounted, leading his horse toward the corral. Sadie stepped in her left stirrup and swung her right leg over Sunny's haunches and landed on firm ground. She pulled the reins over the mare's shiny blonde mane admiring again how far she had come since the day at the kill pen.

"Let me help you there," a male voice interrupted. Sadie turned around to see Justin.

"Thanks, since I don't know what to do out here."

He led his horse toward the corral, and Sadie followed. He led his horse in, and she stayed outside the gate. Justin adeptly removed his horse's headstall to allow the horse to graze without a bit in its mouth and also not step on its reins. He loosened up the cinch on the saddle to give his horse a break around the belly. He did all of this in less than one minute.

"Your turn." He motioned for her to come in.

Sadie brought Sunny in and fumbled with the un-familiar headstall. She had Western tack at home, but not like this.

Justin came closer and said, "Here you go," removing the leather contraption with one hand.

"Thanks," she said, embarrassed. "I'll get the girth — I mean — the cinch." And she did, with success.

"I knew what you meant. Hey, as soon as I'm wrapped up here, you wanna grab lunch? There aren't many of you, so this shouldn't take long."

"Sure," she said, seeing Sunny walk away and remembering she had forgotten to pull out her lunch. "I'll wait for you outside the gate."

Justin went to help the other guests along with Kitty, Levi, and Luke.

Sadie waited for one of those minutes Justin wouldn't be looking and made her way to Sunny who munched the soft green grass, unthreatened by Sadie's approach. She patted her neck and pulled the sack lunch out of her saddlebag. Fortunately, her lunch partner was busy and didn't notice her stupid mistake. She made her way outside the gate.

"Howdy, partner," Austin said, sauntering up to Sadie like a cowboy. She loved her goofy brother. "If you don't mind, Kitty offered to show me and Leah the spring. I figured Leah, as the former soldier, could use the healing waters after wartime like Dad. And I could definitely use the hike."

"Of course I don't mind. With all these nice people here, I'll find something to do."

"Mighty obliged, ma'am." He tilted his cowboy hat at her and smiled.

Why did she tell that little white lie? She didn't have much time to think about it before Justin appeared and said, "Let's go."

Sadie fell in step and wondered why he was in such a rush. She looked back to see Luke exiting the corral and yelling, "Hey!"

Justin turned back to Luke who pointed at his eyes and then pointed to the two of them. Justin said, "Oh, boy. It's not like I don't know the rules."

"What rules?" Sadie asked when they were farther away.

"We're not allowed to get involved with guests. Ranch policy."

"That seems like a stupid rule." She thought about all the girls who must come through here in a season, and then it didn't seem like such a stupid rule to her.

"I don't make the rules, and sometimes I barely follow them, like you found out at the camp."

"Is he still mad at you because of me?"

"Yeah, that and a million other things. Let's talk

about something else." They made their way down a narrow trail, and he pointed for them to take the path to the right. It was moist under the tree cover, with the scent of honeysuckle. It reminded Sadie of a fairytale enchanted forest. Ahead of them in the clearing, a sensational vista appeared. "We're here," he said and patted a rock formation that doubled as a natural bench.

"Wow," was all Sadie managed.

"I thought you might like it. Let's eat; I'm starving."

How could he not react to this? Sadie felt like such a city slicker.

They pulled out their lunches and laughed about how Keela had packed enough food for the people and the horses. He said how much he liked Keela and that everyone did. As they bantered and made small talk, Sadie wondered how many other people, well girls, he'd brought here. Was that why Luke did that thing with the fingers and the eyes saying he was watching?

"Did you hear me?"

"Sorry, no, I was thinking about something else. What was that?"

"I asked you to tell me something you've never told anyone else," he said and took a bite of his sandwich.

"Really? Why?"

"Because I want to know something about you other people don't."

It sounded like a trap to Sadie. But she was only here for three more days, and she couldn't be involved with him anyway. Not that she would know what that was because she hadn't had a boyfriend yet. She said something that had been on her mind lately.

"I'm still one of the few people I know who has a mom and a dad who are married for the first time. I want to help save that in any way I can by not being the problem."

"What would make you think you would be the problem?"

"Something's always the problem."

"Why are we out here talking about parents and problems? You're not the same as the other rich girls," Justin said.

"Maybe because we're not rich."

"If you're here, you're rich in our eyes. We make as much all summer as it costs your family to be here for less than a week."

"Then, why don't you do something else?" Sadie asked.

"Maybe I don't want to be rich. I want to do this. And besides, what other job has this view?"

Sadie scanned the mountains and said, "I can't argue with that. I've seen a lot of places traveling with the military moves, but never anything like it."

"That's because there is nothing like it."

Sadie said, "I have a question for you. What was that

thing you did when you tapped your chest when I was leaving your camp? Was it some kind of code?"

"Code? You mean like Luke's stupid eyes thing? No, not at all. I'm nothing like him. It was my way of saying your heart is in the right place, Sadie. It's a good thing." His face flushed red.

Sadie looked away so he wouldn't see her face show the same color, and a small fast-moving object caught her eye. The rust-colored body hovered over the bush in front of them and tasted a blossom's nectar. "A hummingbird! Another first! And I've definitely never seen one that color, not even in a picture. Look at that orange throat."

Sadie heard the high-pitched whirring of the tiny creature's beating wings.

"There's a lot of them here," Justin said. "Supposedly they travel through. They don't spook the horses."

Sadie said, "I did a school project on hummingbirds once and learned all about them. I didn't pick the subject but was fascinated by them. Some migrate south for weeks straight across the Gulf of Mexico without stopping, following their natural instincts. In ancient times of what's now Mexico and Central America, the hummingbird meant love." She sounded like her favorite teacher, Mr. Edwards, and felt girlish for rambling on about something a cowboy probably could care less about.

"I never thought of a bird as having a meaning. Well,

except for the bald eagle." He focused on the bird and continued, "Maybe a hummingbird represents people in love going on a journey. What do you think?"

Flustered, Sadie asked, "Where?" How stupid.

"Does it matter?" He waited for an answer watching her and not the tiny bird that had moved along.

"I guess not. It could be a big journey or a small journey. Like my parents coming here." There, that was better.

"Or people going on a trail ride," Justin said, and stood and smiled. "C'mon, I'm having fun with you. Let's get back before people think we may have flown off somewhere."

Sadie had her breath back and forced a smile. "I promise not to tell anyone the tough ranch hand was talking about hummingbirds." And love, she thought, but didn't say it out loud.

As Justin led the way back to join the others, he said over his shoulder, "By the way, that's the Rufous Hummingbird. He was a male, and they are supposed to be aggressive. So be careful."

"Of a hummingbird?" Sadie asked. No answer. This Justin was different.

CHAPTER 21

GHOST STORIES

FOR THE ENTERTAINMENT THAT night, the MacKenneys brought in local talent. The acts varied from Cody reciting cowboy poetry to a local girl dressed in a red gingham dress and patent leather shoes playing spoons to make music. Sadie never saw someone play spoons creating folksy melodies with metal utensils slapped against hands, thighs, and surfaces. Stomping feet provided percussive sounds. She wasn't going to try her hand at it but respected the precocious girl wearing bows in her pigtails. She ended with a curtsy to the audience.

On the Navarros' walk back to the cabin, they discussed the spectacular days they all had. Sadie didn't want the day to be over. "Anyone interested in going to the cowboy fire Mr. Mac mentioned on the first day and hearing wranglers tell ghost stories?"

"Are you kidding?" Austin asked.

Mom laughed and said, "I was thinking the same thing. I'm beat, and tomorrow's another full day. I'm lucky if I make it to bed."

"I'm with her," Dad said, putting his arm around Mom's shoulders.

"Sweetheart, I'd love to, but these old bones need a rest," her grandmother answered. "You've met most of the people here. You'll find friends there. If not, make new ones."

"That's more like you, Dad, and Austin. I'm not like the rest of you guys, except you're right about the people here. I'll know someone, and if I don't, I've met all the wranglers. So at least I'll know the storyteller."

Dad turned to Mom and whispered in her ear, "Is it all right for her to go alone?"

"We heard you, Dad," Austin said. "You never did master the whisper."

"It'll be fine, Jim. It's right around the corner, and we've seen how safe this place is. It's not her fault we're a bunch of deadbeats."

Sadie didn't think she needed to ask permission; this was a ranch-sanctioned event that Mr. Mac mentioned on the first night. The conversation turned to other topics like what everyone would do tomorrow. When they arrived at their cabin, Sadie left to walk Grandma to her cabin and said her quick goodbye. She didn't want to press the issue, even though she considered it dumb if her dad would have stopped her from going.

At the Helena cabin, Sadie kissed Grandma on the cheek and said, "Goodnight, Grandma, love you."

"Love you, too, baby girl, and remember a ghost story you can tell me later."

"Will do!" Sadie trotted down the steps and headed in the direction she remembered the Miners Hollow campfire to be in from both the directional signs and the map. It felt good to be free out here in this foreign land right in the U.S. of A. The crickets chirped, frogs croaked, and humans laughed in the distance.

She didn't need to follow signs anymore. A bright blaze shone in a stone circle, and the familiar scent of burning wood led the way. Sadie felt self-conscious entering alone when all eyes seated around the fire turned in her direction. Scanning the faces, she didn't find Pamela's, which she had hoped to. The Canadian Five were having drinks and chatting.

"Sit anywhere you want, Sadie," Rusty said. "I'm about to start a story you won't want to miss."

"Where's your grandma?" Heather asked.

"She's beat. Just me tonight."

"Well, come sit with us. We don't bite." Heather tapped the seat next to her.

Relieved, Sadie said, "Thanks. I'm not as fun as my

grandma, but I'm quieter." Grandma had met almost every guest, having the time of her life. She loved telling and retelling the story about Sadie and the rescue horses and her surf club's sponsorship of Sunny. An Irish storyteller, Grandma made any story exciting.

Rusty spoke in a deep, low voice, "This here story is said to have happened not far from here. Everyone swears it's true. If you're the type who scares easily, you may want to leave so as not to get too spooked."

"Bring it on!" an older gentlemen Sadie didn't know said from across the fire. He must have been from the Bad Guys group. He brought a crispy marshmallow on a stick to his mouth and blew on it.

The wrangler started, "So one night, an old rancher went out to check on an unusual noise coming from his cow barn ... like wailing..." His voice trailed off, and Sadie's mind wandered.

What was she doing here? She didn't like ghost stories. Austin used to tell her ghost stories when she was too young for them. She would never forget the time he told her the scariest story about someone who reached up from a grave. That night, as she fell asleep in her room, a hand reached out from under her bed and grabbed her arm. Sadie screamed. Her brother laughed. She never listened to his scary stories again. Big brothers could be so mean.

She checked faces again and confirmed she was the

only teenager there and out of place. She admitted to herself she also hoped Justin might be there, even if it didn't make sense. Why was she so obsessed with someone she hardly knew? She needed to get over it.

Then again, she could also adjust her plan and visit the other campfire — the ranch hands campfire. She remembered how she started out apprehensive but ended up having more fun over there than she was having here. She wasn't welcome at the camp again. But maybe she could catch Justin's eye, and he could meet her outside the camp. He'd said he wanted to talk more, right? He said he wanted to hear about the rescue, and they didn't talk about it the last time with all the entertainment. The help couldn't fraternize with guests, so she'd be safe, right? It was worth a try. What did she have to lose?

CHAPTER 22

⟜

VISIONS

SADIE WAITED UNTIL RUSTY finished his story but missed most of it while plotting what she would do next. With her aversion to ghost stories, she convinced herself it was better that way.

"Who's next?" he asked.

Sadie stood, and Rusty said, "Go ahead, I'd love to hear one about vampires and zombies you kids are so crazy about these days!"

"Oh, no, not me. Sorry about that. I stood up to leave. I've had enough scare for one night." Probably true, had she listened. "Goodnight, all, see you tomorrow." The group bid farewells, and Sadie traced her steps out the way she came.

Heading in the direction of Justin's camp, the bright moon lit the way, brighter than the moon the first night when she and Austin returned to their cabin. Yes, she definitely looked forward to seeing Justin again tonight. Alone in the woods, she appreciated not hearing Rusty's full story. The cool air chilled her away from the fire.

"Oouuuu…" something howled in the distance. They were wolves, not coyotes, this time. She hadn't heard them at the other campfire. Were they telling her to turn back? No, she read too much into it. Her subconscious must have been processing part of the ghost story and playing tricks on her.

She got closer to the camp and images of Luke's glare the first night popped into her head. His warnings to Justin replayed reminding her she wasn't welcome. She remembered the way he scoffed at her today. She should have thought about all this back at the ghost story fire pit.

Maybe Luke left the camp some nights. Yes, that was it. As the lead ranch hand, he had more to do than to watch teenagers who didn't need watching. How else would he have been at the rodeo?

She shuddered remembering that experience which was bad timing since she had just arrived at the Cowboy Camp.

She heard noises — different noises from the first night — not singing and instruments. Out here, sounds rang clear without competing background noises like cars or sirens. She recognized the same sounds from last night's rodeo. Were they watching it on a phone? Or some kind of TV? No, the sounds were too vivid and loud to be behind a screen.

She heard clapping. Staying behind the area Luke saw her on the first night to stay hidden, she eyed the campfire burning with no one there, a strange scene. She listened to detect the direction of the noise.

Not wanting to stroll through the campfire as an uninvited guest, she picked a path through the woods, careful not to trip or break a branch and be discovered. Not far from the fire, lights shone through the trees, and she closed in on the sounds. She worked her way around to stay hidden but still be able to see. A ranch hand rode in the sand arena that Sadie didn't know was part of the camp. It made sense they'd work and train the horses. But why so late at night?

Luke barked something unintelligible. Sadie squinted because she didn't want to move any closer. She realized she wasn't going to catch Justin's eye with this set-up. What had she been thinking anyway?

Then she saw it — a bucking bronco. Doug swung his arm around wildly trying to stay on. He crashed to the ground with a whump followed by a grunt. He rolled away fast to escape the terrorized horse's thrashing hooves. Luke screamed, "Eight seconds, you idiot! Not five! You told me you could ride! And I don't want to hear any sniveling from you."

Luke pointed to Carlos who pulled a flank strap off the exhausted and seemingly confused horse. Sadie recognized the horse, Reckless, the horse in training Mr. Mac rode in the clinic.

She rubbed her eyes. She had to be wrong. This couldn't be that mellow Mustang mare.

"That horse barely bucked! Mac gets these trash BLM horses that are good for nothing except the kill pen." Luke spat slimy brown tobacco chew on the dirt.

Her stomach tightened; her heart pounded. Sadie didn't grasp what was happening, but something was wrong. Her head filled with mini white stars, and she blinked to make them go away. Abandoning her stupid idea about coming to find Justin, she turned and left, yearning the warmth and security of her cabin and a return to normalcy. Where was Justin? He couldn't be part of whatever was going on.

Sadie hightailed it home; she had taken a wrong turn tonight to the Cowboy Camp. She tried to think of anything to take her mind off being out there alone, in the dark, with wild animals, and something unexplainable. Her collection of delicate white porcelain horses came to mind and how she used to make up fantasy scenes. They would play in a meadow, and a miniature version of her would hop on them bareback in her child world. She longed for those times.

She also remembered how the family cat jumped up on her dresser and knocked over her prized collection, breaking a few of her horses apart. She glued them back together, crooked legs and all. And that's what she needed to do. She needed to figure out a way to make things right again.

Making her way back proved easier than getting there. Her mind in a fog, she couldn't find her cabin key and was happy to find the door unlocked. Her *happy* turned *unhappy* when she found her father had waited up for her.

She exhaled, trying not to let him hear her fear. "Hi, Dad."

"Hi, baby. I tried to go to sleep, but I couldn't. I'm glad you're home. You look spooked. Everything okay?"

She had no idea what she had seen. Yes, she was spooked, but not by the ghost stories. She didn't want him to worry about her. She wanted him to think of her as mature. In her steadiest voice for the time, she said, "I'm tired, that's all."

"Me, too. But I couldn't sleep because I needed to talk to you. Have a seat." He patted the chair next to him, and she sat in the empty chair and crossed her arms waiting for the lecture. "You probably get mad at me the way I'm protective at times. I can't help it. I saw horrible things in Afghanistan I don't like to talk about.

But that doesn't mean those pictures in my mind have been erased. They're still there."

Puzzled, she asked, "What does that have to do with me?"

Dad explained, "I want to protect you. I don't want things to happen to you like what happened to those girls; those visions are with me. I want the best for you. You have opportunities they didn't, and I'll never forget that. I feel I owe it to them."

Sadie wanted her father to go on because he never talked about his time at war last year. He claimed he was fine, but he was different. "Dad, I'm sorry, but I'm having a hard time understanding what girls in Afghanistan have to do with me in Montana."

He turned, sighed, and looked her in the eye. "I want you to be safe. I know you are fourteen and think you are all grown up, but you are still my little girl. And you always will be."

She thought about confiding in her dad about what she may have seen but was too unsure of herself. Instead, she stared down to the floorboards wishing she could crawl under them. "Thank you, Dad." She couldn't feel any worse.

CHAPTER 23

RIDE TO THE LAKE

THE SUN ROSE BRIGHT in that never-ending sky again promising another picturesque Montana day. Sadie watched the wranglers and ranch hands while they finished readying the herd of horses for today's ride. Was her imagination running away with her, or was Doug limping?

Sadie chose the easy ride this morning to be with Grandma. Well, that, and she still felt unbalanced by last night.

She let out a sigh of relief when she heard Luke call, "Those going on the Man from Snowy River Ride, over here with me." Did he sneer? Sadie understood the reference, as did most of the guests. It meant the ride would be like the iconic scene from the movie *The Man from*

Snowy River where it portrayed a rough and tumble ride down a steep, rocky side of a mountain. Sadie was relieved Luke would not be on her ride. She didn't like to be near him; he gave her the creeps.

Grandma asked, "Are you sure you don't want to go with them? It may be the chance of a lifetime? I'm okay; my friends are here." She nodded in the direction of her Canadian herd.

"No!" Sadie answered, a bit too sharp. She backpedaled. "I mean, no, Grandma, I want to ride with you. Some of my rides on Lucky were as tough as that one, I'm sure."

"Not the same Lucky I picked out for you. He's been an absolute angel around me."

Sadie thought back to her early days with Lucky when she learned the hard way how demanding it was to train a young colt. She thought back to the many times he dumped her in the dirt from his antics, never mean antics, only the result of baby horse behavior. Smiling back at her grandmother, she said, "Yes, Grandma, he's an angel most of the time. Anyhow, the answer is no, I already signed up for this ride and don't want to mess anything up."

"Nonsense, if you want to change your mind, I can talk to Mac. He'll make it happen," Grandma said.

"No doubt, but you're stuck with me." She flashed the peace sign.

Wrangler Levi said, "Anna, Sweetie's waiting for you, or should we rename her something more surfer themed?" By now, everyone knew Grandma's story. While some kids might have been embarrassed by an outgoing, personable grandmother, Sadie appreciated the attention people lavished on her.

"Sadie?" Justin asked. "You ready?"

Her heart skipped a beat. She expected Justin to be with Luke, like the other rides. She didn't answer and headed toward Sunny.

Justin pulled the reins over Sunny's head and stood to Sunny's left. "Let me give you a leg up like we do out on the trail. You know what you're doing."

"Okay, thanks." She hopped on with ease, glad to be back with her reason to be here once more. She headed out of the corral area and said over her shoulder, "See you out there."

Justin nodded, but he gave her an odd look. Why could everyone read her thoughts? She needed to put on her game face, as Dad called it when they played cards. The two of them always played partners, and Dad tried to teach her not to smile big or frown bigger revealing to the other players what cards she had in her hand. Today she needed her game face for real and was glad she had practiced when it was a game.

The small group of eight headed out on the trail in yet another new direction. Levi had the head, and Justin the tail until they would later split out and no longer ride nose-to-tail. Levi explained they would be taking an easy ride to the lake and assured them it was a better ride than the other. The wranglers competed with each other about whose rides were better, and the groups following played along.

Birds soared way above in the clean and clear air, and Sadie reached out to touch one. She knew the bird was too far away, but something made her do it. It felt right. She reached down and patted Sunny, who craned her neck around, blinking her thick eyelashes. At that second, Sunny reminded her of Esperanza, Spirit's mother in the movie *Spirit: Stallion of the Cimarron*. Wasn't that movie supposed to have been set somewhere out here in the West? She savored the moment of nonreality.

Grandma rode up beside her when the trail got wider, and said, "Penny for your thoughts."

"Nothing you haven't heard before. About the rescue, and how it shouldn't be a big deal. I mean, what else was I supposed to do? I'm no heroine who soared down from the sky destined to save the world. I did what was right." She dismissed that thought and continued, "But most of all, I'm thinking about how I'm so happy Sunny found a good home and likes her job. And a lot of it is because of you. Your club sponsored her. Now look at her!" She pointed to the lovely palomino plodding along like she had done this her whole life. For some reason, Sadie fought back tears. She hated showing her emotional side.

"Well, you started it, so there!" Grandma laughed. "Think about the future. How many people will get to ride her and enjoy her? How many people who don't own horses like you do will get to ride her for a whole week and never forget her. I can tell she's going to be a ranch favorite. She'll show up in people's pictures from all over the world and end up in those photos on their phones and in their homes for years."

"I don't think she cares about the pictures, Grandma." Heather's words "a hoot" came to mind.

"Speaking of pictures, let me take one of you and her." Grandma steered obedient Sweetie to the right. While walking in tandem, she snapped a burst of photos. These horses didn't flinch at the sound, used to tourists and camera sounds, unlike certain high-strung show horses Sadie had seen.

"There's bound to be a good one somewhere. It's not hard when a movie star model rides a movie star of a horse."

Sadie blushed. "You noticed she looked like Esperanza, too?"

"Who's Esperanza? I was thinking of Trigger."

"Esperanza, from the movie *Spirit*, Spirit's mom."

Levi called from the front in that way he rode forward and turned around with his right hand on the back of the saddle at the same time. "Hey, Anna, come on up here, if you can."

"Oh, can we catch up on this later?" Grandma asked. "I asked Levi if he would point out the cave when we got close. There're legends about gold hidden there by bank robbers. I told you outlaws came here! He said we're not going to ride to the cave, but I could get a picture from a distance. I can't miss this!"

Grandma. Caves. Legends. No surprises. Sadie enjoyed the silence except the background conversations of the other riders. She spent so much time with her family, Pamela, the other guests, and Justin, that she had little time to reflect. At home, she had quiet time, especially when riding Lucky alone. That was her favorite time.

"You okay?" Justin asked, having taken Grandma's place to Sadie's right.

"Um, yeah," Sadie answered, concentrating on her game face.

"What's wrong? You seem, I don't know … distant?"

"Lost in thought is all." Then she quizzed him: "So, what do you know about Luke?" No game face in the world could recover from that one. Open mouth, insert foot, they say. She would never make it as a spy.

Justin gazed off ahead taking his time to answer. "Not much. He's an experienced rider, or they wouldn't have hired him."

"Where did he come from?"

"Montana somewhere."

"Do you know anything else?"

"He likes to win, that's for sure."

Well, so did Sadie. This was going nowhere. "Don't you wonder about the person you're working for? I mean, I work a volunteer job, and I know lots about my boss, Ms. Kristy."

"Well, Ms. Kristy may be warmer and fuzzier than a hardened ranch hand. For us, it's not about getting to know you; it's more about getting to work," he shared a crooked smile with her.

He gazed off again. He was hiding something. She could spot a liar.

They rode in silence down a long, rolling hill where the lake they came to see emerged on their right. Behind it, monumental rocks pointed to the sky, and water trickled down to the sparkling pool at the bottom. The lake spread the expanse of at least ten football fields. The water rippled from bugs skimming the surface and fish beneath finding their unsuspecting next snacks.

"Another day at work for me. Isn't it beautiful?" Justin asked.

Sadie snapped out of her trance. "You keep talking about the beauty of the scenery? What about the beauty of the horses?"

Justin stared at her, then down to his hand on his knee, right where a cowboy's hand should be. "You're acting weird. I'm not sure what's gotten into you, but I seem to be bothering you. That's not our job. We're supposed to help you have a good time, and that's not happening. I'm sorry about whatever it is I did to you to make you feel this way. I'll be on my way."

She met his eyes again, and this time she didn't see deceit. She saw hurt. Had she read him wrong? All he'd done was try to be nice. And she's holding something against him that she may or may not have seen and he may or may not know about. After all, she hadn't seen him there. Justin tipped his hat and rode off to talk to another guest who might appreciate his hospitality. She was so confused.

Grandma passed Justin while heading back to Sadie, greeting every guest along the way by name. She reached

Sadie and said, "I saw you talking to your friend." She winked an exaggerated wink.

Sadie let out a heavy sigh. "Yeah," she paused and had a thought. "Grandma, do you think I can spend the night tonight? You said you wanted to do a bunk night one night."

"I was waiting for you to ask! And you can tell me the ghost story you promised from last night."

"Then we have a deal." Sadie was afraid the real story she would share with her would be scarier than any of the ghost stories Rusty told last night.

CHAPTER 24

CHECKING IN

BACK IN THE CABIN after lunch, Sadie dialed Brady for another check-in at the time they'd set up. He was at the barn attending to Lucky. When Brady answered the phone, the screen showed Lucky's face, sort of, more like his nostrils. Sadie recognized the view.

"Hi, Brady, or is this Lucky answering the phone?" Sadie asked.

Brady turned the phone around to himself and said, "Both of us, I figured you wanted to see him more than me."

"Not exactly. I can talk to him, but he won't talk back to me. How's everything?"

"All is well, and I think Lucky may have gained a few pounds with all the treats he's been getting. See the sign I made?" He pointed the camera to a handwritten sign on Lucky's stall that read, "Extra treats allowed. My mom's not here, and I miss her."

"How cute!" She thought about the words. She used the same word that got her so upset at Blake on day one. It didn't seem so bad now with time.

"Although everyone knew you were gone, with the sign, everyone is stopping by to give Lucky an extra pat and a treat. It's like I'm not needed anymore."

"What horsekeeper would say that? Besides, he needs you. Those folks may know their way to his belly, but you're the one who knows the way to his heart."

"I guess you're right." He entered Lucky's stall using one hand for the door and the other for the phone. Sadie tried not to get seasick from all the motion. Once inside, he turned the phone to show both of them and scratched Lucky under his jaw where he showed his appreciation by stretching out his neck.

Sadie asked, "What's new, anything?"

"Not really. Pretty much the same ole same ole. Oh, the picture your Grandma took of you and Sunny looks like you should be in a magazine! Maybe one day you and I can go to Montana. What do you think?" He smiled, forgetting about Lucky's scratches.

"Yeah, why not?"

Lucky pushed Brady with his nose, notifying him

he wanted more. He scratched him with one hand and looked straight into the phone. "Are you okay?"

"Yeah, why?"

"You seem … off."

She changed the subject. "Where's Hope?"

"She went to a birthday party I wasn't invited to." He paused and surveyed Lucky, as if seeking guidance. "Sadie, I thought we were friends. Something's wrong, and I thought you could trust me." His little eyebrows pulled together.

"You *are* my friend." Which was exactly why she couldn't tell him some cockamamie story about last night and make him worry. "Everything's different here, and sometimes I couldn't be happier, and other times I'm like a fish out of water. You know what I mean?"

"I know all about being a fish out of water. And you've always helped me find that water."

He was so sweet. All she did was try to be his friend. "That, and I miss Lucky and home. But I'm better after talking to you and seeing Lucky." She forced a smile. "See?"

"You look better."

"Are you looking forward to being Ms. Kristy's horse program assistant without me today?" She saw his face blanch. "You didn't forget, did you? Today is Thursday."

"Honestly, I did forget. I've been so busy taking care of Lucky, I haven't thought about much else. Good thing you called!"

Sadie thought for a minute. "Good thing you didn't go to that party. Ms. Kristy's horse kids would have been so disappointed if you weren't there." Sadie read her friend like a book, and from the few words he said about the party, he was hurt. He was the most sensitive boy she'd ever met.

"You're right! Poor Ms. Kristy, what would she have done if both of us weren't here? You're saving the day from across the country."

"Well, now that we settled that, let me say goodbye to Lucky. I have a lesson this afternoon I need to get ready for." She thought she'd share with him about her new friend, Pamela, who was taking a lesson with her today but decided it could wait until she got home. There he was taking care of her horse, and here she was gallivanting across the countryside and meeting international friends. Yes, it could wait.

Brady turned the phone to Lucky's face and said in a funny voice she assumed was his version of Lucky, "I miss you, Mom." Brady's real voice followed. "I hope you find your water in the next few days. You deserve to be happy."

"Thank you, and I'll be back soon. I won't bug you again, but please call me if anything happens."

"You know I would," he answered. "And it's not just Lucky who misses you; I do, too."

⌐

CHAPTER 25

PIONEER
PARTNERS

GRANDMA'S HELENA CABIN SMELLED of potpourri, fresh-cut wood, and a light scent of her tea rose perfume. It was like being in a forest and a rose garden at the same time. Sadie couldn't place the unknown scent.

"What is that spicy smell? And why doesn't our cabin smell like that?"

"It's patchouli, my dear, supposed to be soothing and ward off evil spirits. I had choices." In the small kitchen, she opened a drawer containing fragrant potpourri blends. The choices included pine, which Sadie didn't understand because it already smelled like wood; cranberry, too sweet; and vanilla, too bland. Grandma made the right choice.

"I suspect your mom didn't go hunting around

cupboards like I did. You know me, always curious. Funny, your mom's the one who went into the intelligence field. If times had been different, that would have been me."

"Interesting you bring that up, Grandma." Sadie wondered how she was going to broach the subject she wanted to talk to her about. "I could use your sleuth skills."

Grandma's eyes got wide. "Really? She looked around, locked the door, and whispered, "What's going on?"

They sat at her table with natural burls in the wood still visible under the varnish and shellac. Sadie bit her lower lip, an annoying habit, and started: "I don't know where to begin. But first, you need to promise you won't think I'm crazy."

"Promise," she said and made the motion of a cross over her heart with her right hand.

Sadie drummed her fingers on the surface trying to make her thoughts come out while making sense, knowing this was her only hope. "Last night, I left after the first ghost story when I remembered how much I hated ghost stories. Since I was out, I decided to stop by the camp where Austin and I went the other night." She waited for admonishment.

Instead, Grandma said, "And..."

Sadie spared her the details of the harrowing trip there and the wolves howling and dove into the meat of the story. "When I got there, I think I saw something I shouldn't have. I'm not sure what it was. But I heard that nasty Luke yelling, and the sweet mustang, Reckless, looked so scared, no ... confused ... or defeated. Then one of the ranch hands got thrown off hard. It wasn't right."

"What did they say when you showed up? It couldn't be all that bad if they're doing whatever they're doing in front of guests."

"True, but they didn't see me because Luke made it clear after the first night guests were not welcome. So I hid. It seems stupid, but I was hoping to see Justin. Instead, I'm afraid of what I might have stumbled into."

Grandma sat silent and drew a pattern into one of the table's wooden swirls. "Let's go through the five Ws to help figure this out." Grandma remembered that from when they solved the mystery of Lucky's disappearance a few years ago. Grandma grabbed the pad of stationery and the pen left for guests in the cabins and wrote the word "Who" on the page. "*Who's* involved?"

"Luke for sure, and some of the horses, although I don't think they want to be. At least a few of the ranch hands are involved, like the one who hit the ground last night."

"Okay, and *what*? What do you think they are doing? Sorry you have to answer all the questions. I'll try to help as I can, but I'm at a disadvantage, not having been there."

"You're already helping by listening. I haven't told anyone, and it's been bottled up so bad inside me I want to burst. I don't know the 'what.' It seemed like training, but these horses don't need to buck like that."

"Like at the rodeo?" Grandma asked, hand on her chin.

The words came out slow, "Like - at - the - rodeo." Sadie's mind spun with visions of the town rodeo. "Oh my God, Grandma, it's beginning to make sense! Luke. The rodeo. The plan!"

"I'm afraid you're losing me. I may be a good sleuth, but I need a clue or two."

"I didn't tell you this part yet. At the rodeo the other night, I overheard Luke talking to a guy who came looking for him because Luke owes people money. Luke said he had 'a plan,' but the plan was going to take time. Maybe the plan is he's going to use the ranch hands to make him money at some rodeo! But first he needs to finish training them and get them to practice, so they can win."

"So you were spying at the town rodeo, too? How did you suspect something was wrong then, and how did you keep that secret in?"

"I didn't spy or suspect anything. I came across it as one piece of a puzzle I didn't understand. The pieces are coming together. It makes sense the ranch hands couldn't compete on a Tuesday night at the Settlers Rodeo since Mr. Mac and other wranglers would be there. But that doesn't mean they couldn't compete on a weekend night or in other local rodeos."

"Let's go tell Mac and your parents. This is serious." Grandma's happy-go-lucky demeanor disappeared.

"No! We can't do that! These are all my guesses, with no proof. If we go to anyone with this, it will look like me being a big snoop. They'll ask me what I was doing at the rodeo sneaking around, and why I was at the Cowboy Camp last night. I can't tell them it's because I have a crush on one of the ranch hands I'm not allowed to like."

Grandma nodded, reached across the table, and squeezed Sadie's hand. Grandma remembered being a fourteen-year-old girl. "I understand more than you know. All the ideas are theories, and they're loose. Let's go back to our mystery-solving formula and keep working. The next W is *when*."

"I can answer *when* and *where* at the same time. If they are doing this, they will be practicing at the same place tonight, at the same time," Sadie said in a voice calmer than the nerves coursing through her veins.

Grandma said, "We have one idea about *why*. Let's go see what we can do. We need to collect evidence."

She pulled out her cell phone and said, "We have our collection tool right here. We sneak in, grab a shot and a video or two, and we're on our way. Easy peasy."

Sadie didn't agree with the easy part; however, she had to do something. It was the best plan at the time.

"Okay, but let's plan an alibi," Sadie said the word like it rolled off her tongue every day. "If anyone stops us, we're out taking photographs of the stars and the moon. Got it?"

"That's my girl! Always thinking. Let's get in dark clothes; we don't want to be standing out." Grandma rummaged through her drawers. "I guess you look okay as you are. I'm the one who needs to hide better," she said, looking down at the blingy yellow outfit she still wore from the day. "And one last thing … thank you for trusting me."

"Of course, Grandma, we're partners, always."

CHAPTER 26

THE OTHER RODEO

SADIE AND GRANDMA MADE their way to the camp on their covert mission with the moonlight and stars lighting the way. They silenced their phones before arriving at the scene where the lighted arena stood out.

Sadie began videoing the scene, not sure what the camera would capture. It didn't take long before she watched in horror as the massive Comanche exploded out of a jerry-rigged chute. The sweet, calm horse Justin had ridden on the trail bucked furiously trying to eject Carlos. What had happened? What did they do to him? And why? She heard her answer.

"Hang on, cowboy, or you ain't gonna win a dime! Balance, balance — think about what you're doing! You need to win me money, boy, for all this work I'm putting into you. Of course, you probably don't understand a word I'm saying."

Carlos hung on as Comanche bucked and turned in unnatural positions trying to unseat him and make whatever was making him hurt stop hurting. Sadie remembered learning about bucking straps. But that was for rodeo horses, not for family-friendly ranch horses. And didn't Blake say you can't make horses buck? They bred and trained them for it, right?

Sadie recognized the same look on Comanche as she had seen on Reckless, utter confusion and fear as to what they did wrong to deserve this. Carlos hopped off after a makeshift buzzer sounded, and he led Comanche away, who still appeared rattled. This was outright animal cruelty.

"Keep working at it. This guy was easy. Okay, Miss Kitty, your turn to show us what you got tonight."

Kitty shot out of the starting area on Sunny. Sunny! Sadie wasn't sure she could control herself, shocked to see her mare involved. Kitty rode Sunny better than any of the barrel riders she saw at the rodeo. But Sadie saw the whites in Sunny's eyes from all the way out where they were and through the lens of a phone camera. Sunny appeared scared to death. Kitty rounded the first barrel and headed to the second squeezing the mare on with her legs. At least she didn't wear gigantic spurs.

Sunny tried to round the second barrel and plowed through it instead. The sound and commotion spooked her, and Kitty barely hung on as the barrel tipped. Most of the ranch hands laughed, and Sadie couldn't stop thinking about what poor Sunny must have been experiencing. Luke shouted, telling Kitty what to do and insulting her.

Sadie peeked away from her video for a moment to Grandma, who gestured to the arena like they should do something. Sadie shook her head as if she knew what she was doing. She didn't, but she needed more evidence. Grandma nodded, and gave her the shh sign, which for some reason relieved her.

Sunny got through the barrel pattern and passed the starting area. Kitty jogged her back in with the mare's head hung low. Sunny's eyes stayed open wide, and her nostrils flared. She shook.

Grandma mouthed the words to Sadie, "You were right!"

Kitty encouraged Sunny and soothed her by stroking her neck, looking down at Luke. "There, girl, nice and easy, you did fine."

"She did not do fine — that sucked! They'd laugh you out of the rodeo for that, unless you're supposed to be the clown," he said. The cowboys laughed, except Justin. Sadie kept her eyes on Justin, wondering what he thought of this situation. He seemed uncomfortable. Was it for Kitty or the horse?

Kitty raised her voice. "I told you, she's not a barrel horse. It's how she got hurt. You know we can't train them to do this overnight."

So that's why she was lame.

Luke continued, "I don't need to train the horse. I need to train *you*. I got a horse you're gonna ride, but you can't ride her 'til the rodeo. That horse will do what she's supposed to do. You told me you could ride, but from what I keep seeing, you can't."

"That's not true. I've got more buckles and wins than anyone here except you! I can't help it if my mom sold my horse and left. I'm trying to earn money to buy her back. Do you know how that feels?" It sounded like Kitty knew something of Luke's story.

"We're getting bored out here," Cash said.

"Shut up, you. And Miss Kitty, run her again. Do it right this time." Luke walked away and spit.

Sadie continued to video the scene. This had to be torture for Sunny. She wanted to please, and she couldn't, because she didn't know how to.

The next round was worse. Kitty dismounted.

"This is not the way to train her, and not with these ninnies around clapping, getting her all riled up. I don't need to practice anyway. I'll ride your barrel mare, and I'll win. Seeing the competition in this town, I'll show them."

"Who's in charge here? Get your head in the game, girl. This here is an animal, and animals have to listen to people. Let me show you how I learned to do it."

Luke grabbed a bullwhip torture instrument from the arena sideline. He raised it in the air, and Kitty put herself between the brutal whip's tail and Sunny. Luke pulled it away just in time.

"Don't think I won't. You got lucky this time. Get that animal out of my sight. You, too. I should have known better than to hire a girl hand."

Kitty glared at him and turned around to lead Sunny away, both heads down. Luke raised the whip again, and Sadie screamed, "Stop!" She put her hand to her mouth too late.

"Who's out there?" Luke asked, in a cringe-worthy voice.

"Only us, young man. We're out here taking some night photographs since we don't have stars like this where we come from," Grandma said, not convincingly.

Luke shined a flashlight in Sadie's eyes, blinding her. She put her free hand up to shield her eyes. "And you," Luke hissed. "I should have known."

Sadie's heart beat out of her chest; she hoped Luke

couldn't see her shaking from a distance. This had been a bad plan.

Luke turned to the three ranch hands still there. She couldn't see who they were, still blinded by the light. She knew Kitty kept going when the commotion started. Smart girl. Luke said, "Head on back to the camp now." The kids slinked off leading two more horses away, stealing glances back at what was happening in the woods.

Luke asked, "Why don't you ladies come on over and show me your pictures of the stars?" Sadie couldn't mistake the tone for being anything other than it was: menacing. She looked to Grandma for help.

"Oh, that's okay; it seems we've disturbed something here, so we'll be on our way."

Luke took a step toward them, and Sadie froze in place. She couldn't even look at Grandma. He took another step, and Sadie contemplated racing to escape. He was still at least twenty steps away. But she couldn't leave Grandma there. What would a person who raised a whip to a horse and a girl do to an enemy who threatened his big plan?

CHAPTER 27

OUTLAWS

"WHY DON'T YOU LADIES stay right there? I wouldn't want you tripping in the woods in the dark. That wouldn't be good for Homeplace, would it? You seem off the beaten path."

Sadie and Grandma exchanged glances, but neither spoke. Luke closed the gap between them bounding through the branches breaking under his heavy steps. He was quick, like the bulls at the rodeo.

"I think we'll be going," dauntless Grandma mustered up. "We didn't mean to disturb you and the boys."

"And a girl," came a voice behind Luke. His flashlight continued to blind Sadie, but she recognized Kitty's voice.

Luke turned to her and growled, "What are you doing here?"

"Nothing much. The boys said we had some visitors, and I wanted to make sure we were being hospitable."

With the light out of her eyes for a second, Sadie focused on Kitty's defiant expression.

"Get out of here! No one invited you; like I didn't invite them."

Grandma said, "Like I said, we'll be on our way. Come on, Sadie, and thanks, Miss Kitty, for coming out to check on us. We're fine."

Luke eyeballed Kitty up and down. "Get back to the camp where you belong. Now."

Kitty hesitated but retreated into the shadows. Their witness departed, and they were alone again for whatever came next. Sadie was in way over her head.

"I don't want any trouble, ladies. I want to see your pictures to make sure you didn't photograph something by mistake. I'm sure it's okay with you, isn't it? You see, our horse training is proprietary, meaning protected, and we need to make sure our unique methods don't leave the ranch. I'm sure you understand," Luke said. Sadie didn't believe a word.

Grandma took off into the dark in the direction they came. Oh, Grandma, that bull moved too fast! He'd be on her in no time. Sadie's mind shifted into overdrive. When Luke moved in Grandma's direction, Sadie dove in front of his sprinting feet. How did she know to do that?

Thump! She heard the sound and felt the impact on the ground at the same time. Luke dropped his flashlight which gave Sadie seconds until he found it. She didn't stand a chance against his 200-pound ranch work-hardened frame. She scrambled to her feet and bolted in the direction of the arena, so he would need to decide which way to go. If she picked up her pace, she would reach Kitty and the others. That had to be safer than out here with this madman.

Her adrenaline kicked in; she sprinted with all her might hearing footfalls and heavy breathing close behind her. Good — he had come after her instead of Grandma. Scared out of her mind, she still preferred this outcome considering all this happened because of her ideas. She couldn't look back; she had to keep moving forward, moving faster than the steps closing in behind her with every step.

Then she saw it. The whip. The whip her pursuer tried to use on a horse. On *her* horse — the horse she rescued from potential abuse and slaughter. Sadie swooped down, still at a run, and picked up the evil leather weapon. Could she use it? She summoned up her hate for what he was doing. She had to believe she could use it, or at least believe she could keep Luke from making her his latest victim.

Luke gained on her in the middle of the lighted arena. Sadie had nowhere to hide. She'd been trying to prove how grown up she was all week; she had to prove it to herself. She channeled her thoughts on Sunny, how peaceful she was on their rides, and the fear in her eyes tonight. She had to defend her.

Sadie stopped and turned to face her villain. Shoulders back, whip in hand, she yelled, "Get back!"

"Oh, c'mon, kid? You can't be serious. You don't know how to use that thing." He mocked her which he shouldn't have.

"Oh yeah? I watched how you almost used it on Sunny and Kitty. I'm a quick study." She flicked the long leather whip up and snapped it to the ground with a loud crack. She saw that in movies. She also handled the long-handled longe whips while training Lucky from the ground.

Luke looked stunned.

"Back off and leave me alone," Sadie said, standing tall and feeling small.

"I'm afraid I can't let that happen. You're trespassing in my camp, and that's illegal. Doesn't the map say, 'Off Limits'? Yeah, I can't have that." He took a step forward.

"I said back off!" Empowered, she cracked the whip again. With the reflexes of a rattlesnake, Luke grabbed the tail of the whip in the air. She looked up and saw blood dripping from his palm at the same time she lost balance from the abrupt stop of the whip's momentum. She landed on her back with the wind knocked out of her.

Disoriented, she felt like what she had seen in Reckless on the first night, and in Comanche and Sunny tonight.

Sadie's instincts kicked in, and she threw her hands over her head while on the ground as if she fell from Lucky to guard herself from hooves striking her head. She was about to lose consciousness from the impact of the fall or the stress of the situation; she didn't know which.

A firm female voice announced from the edge of the woods, "Luke Parsons, you can stop right there."

"Says who?" Luke quipped.

"Says Special Agent Leah Mulhall, Cascade County Sheriff's Office. You're under arrest." She came forward to the arena with a gun drawn for protection. She meant business. Although Luke was the scariest person Sadie had confronted, Leah's background told her this was peanuts to her. She had chased terrorists in Afghanistan. This rogue cowboy couldn't intimidate her. "Hands on your head, *now!*" Sadie appreciated her using the "now" term and realized she must have been listening for at least a short time to repeat its meaning.

"Are you all right?" Austin called. "Can we come over yet, Leah? Grandma's going crazy over here talking martial arts and taking care of things," unshakeable Austin said, sounding shaken.

"Give me a minute. This *is* a crime scene, folks. Luke Parsons, you have the right to remain silent..." Sadie listened to the words, but it still didn't register. The handcuffs clinked, and the other ranch hands lined the arena on the side opposite the woods.

"Come on over, but don't touch anything over here." She pointed to the area which apparently was the crime scene. "Sadie, look me in the eye. Can you stand up? Are you okay? Do I need to call an ambulance?"

She jumped up. "No! I'm fine."

She was dizzy, likely more to do with the mental than the physical experience. She nodded she was okay, willing herself not to cry in front of this crowd, mostly in front of the ranch hands. "Are my parents here?" she asked, wanting them to be but also wondering how she would explain all this.

"Not yet. They are all on their way back from the night on the town dancing at the Utica Saloon. I didn't know what was going on until we got here, so I didn't want to alarm them, especially your dad. But don't worry, I posted a watch at the entrance of Homeplace keeping an eye on anyone coming in and out of the facility. You're safe."

Special Agent Mulhall turned to the ranch hands. "That goes for you, too."

She continued to Sadie, "Go on over and thank your brother for saving you from I'm not sure what yet, but definitely not good."

Sadie ran to Austin who had joined them in the arena. She hugged him and let loose the tears she had been holding in, hiding her face in his chest. He patted her back and talked to her like one soothes a horse. Grandma joined in, and the three of them hugged and held together like a tripod saying nothing.

Finally, Austin said, "This was not what I expected. I went to Grandma's cabin, and admit I was going to play a joke trying to scare you for old times' sake. When I didn't find you there, I thought Grandma might have dragged you to the ghost stories fire. You weren't there, but Leah was. Something didn't seem right with you both missing and nothing else to do, so I pulled her aside."

Grandma said, "That's my boy, more good instincts." Her voice quivered.

"I thought this camp would be a place to check, even if they didn't want me here. Leah was happy to be on a mission, and I didn't realize what a mission it would be!"

Sadie asked, "Why didn't you ask Mom and Dad?"

"They were in town. I think this may have been the first date they've been on in over a year without us around. And I didn't think this was what we would find."

"I'll butt in here, too, Sadie," Leah said. "I was out here looking for something and not sure what. I needed to follow all my leads. Your brother turned out to be my best lead."

What? Leads, crime scenes, evidence — this was not how she pictured her ranch trip!

Special Agent Mulhall hollered back to them, "Sorry, but I need to work. I'm going to meet a car waiting at the camp entrance. We'll transport Luke to Great Falls where he'll be charged and arraigned. I'll be back in the morning to take statements and collect evidence. For you ranch hands, my partners can take your statements." She nodded at the three uniformed police who had shown up during the discussion. "And a safety tip, since I've gotten to know you guys, and girl — tell the truth."

The policewoman departed with the man who tried to hurt Sunny. The man who tried to hurt her, too. Leah walked by the ranch hands, and they appeared relieved. Sadie caught Justin's eye, the way she wanted to a few nights ago which led her to this whole nightmare and her suspicions about what may be happening here. She still couldn't believe he would willingly be a part of this.

Justin looked ashamed but had pride enough to say to Sadie on her way out, "Thank you." He tapped his chest twice the way he'd done before in the signal that said her heart was in the right place. She thought she understood his meaning and returned the gesture to him hoping there was more meaning to it. She had to believe his heart was in the right place, too.

⌒

CHAPTER 28

THE UNRAVELING

FRIDAY MORNING, SPECIAL AGENT Mulhall asked Sadie, her parents, and Grandma to meet her in the Homeplace office, the first place they came all those days ago for their keys and cabin assignments. Everything seemed so idyllic when Sadie first arrived. On their way to the office, Mom gave directions. She told Dad and Grandma she'd do the talking for them.

"I won't say a word unless asked," Grandma said.

Dad nodded. He still appeared stunned, shell-shocked, or not sure what to do, which was unusual for him.

Once they settled in the office at a sturdy oak table, Leah shuffled papers and began unraveling the story. It turned out Luke was worse than Sadie realized. Not only the animal cruelty, but he had lured the ranch hands to Montana with promises of fame and fortune. Once they arrived, he trapped them with no way out.

"How did Homeplace hire this Luke person?" Sadie asked her.

"First of all, I can tell you some things, but not others since the investigation isn't over. The first point is that I ended up out here due to a complaint filed to our office."

"Who filed the complaint?" Sadie asked, hoping it was Justin.

"I'm sorry, I can't tell you at this time. But it turned out to be a good tip, for a change. Since you broke up this ring, I need more information from you today, so you're in luck."

In luck? Sadie didn't feel so lucky.

Leah continued after the silence: "Luke wasn't always this bad. Mac knew of him and his rodeo background. It's hard to hire ranch hands and wranglers because of the hard work. He seemed like the right fit.

"But he used inhumane methods to train those horses. The kids are talking to protect themselves. They didn't agree with what he was doing, but they didn't have a say. They were afraid of him, for good reason. The ways he would make those horses buck were old cowboy tricks he'd learned somewhere along the line. They wouldn't be tolerated today."

Sadie's skin crawled at the thought. She wanted details but then again didn't.

"He used the newer, green horses thinking they'd be more likely to be reactive. They were also in training and not as experienced so provided better training for the riders. Not to mention, if the horses showed up lame, it could easily be attributed to them being new at their jobs or in the herd."

Sadie barely listened wondering what someone so abusive to animals would also do to exploit humans. Was Justin a victim? Had Kitty been hurt? What about Carlos? How could people be like that? She would never understand, but she would follow her instincts from here on out.

Maybe her spy mom's intelligence analyst skills ran in the family. Grandma already said the sleuthing started with her and her keen intellect. Maybe Sadie had the family gene.

Leah continued, "Luke had quite the operation going. Three of these kids showed up on the missing persons list."

"What? But they said—"

"They said what Luke told them to say. I'm not saying all their lives were perfect, but they were better off wherever they were than being in this trap. You not only saved the horses he put in danger, but you saved these kids."

What? She didn't come here to save anyone. She came

here to check on a mare. And she almost talked herself out of that in the beginning.

"This is so much bigger than what we expected," Leah said. "Our precinct thought this would be a case of animal neglect or abuse, which turned out to be right. But this also turned into a human trafficking issue. This doesn't happen out here. At least we didn't think so until now."

"What? And what will happen to them … like Justin?" Sadie asked.

"We've contacted Justin's mom who was shocked to hear he was in Montana. She dropped him off at a summer boarding school to get him ahead on his studies. She's been getting weekly emails from him as if everything's fine."

So he had no problem lying. Sadie's heart sunk.

"And Luke was a smart guy," Leah said. "He confiscated their cell phones when they arrived calling it ranch policy. The MacKenneys didn't do that, and I detected something was off from the get-go. What teenager is not looking at a cell phone these days?

"But he was smart enough to let them send one censored message a week, so he controlled the information going out."

Mom asked, "Wouldn't the school contact his mother when he didn't show up?"

"That Justin's a bright one. He wrote to the school

pretending to be his mom and told them to use her new email address. Then he disenrolled but told them to keep the payment due to the late notice. The school corresponded with him a few times, thinking they were talking to her. His mom was in the dark."

Mom shook her head.

"Justin's mother is a big executive in Chicago, a single mom, and sent him to summer camps and boarding schools for years. She had no idea what happened until last night. She's on her way."

Sadie pondered that about his mom. Her mom wondered where she was minutes after she didn't answer a text message. Justin's mom didn't know her son was essentially kidnapped. She tried to clear her mind from that thought and asked, "How did Luke find these kids?"

"Predator."

"Meaning?"

"He set up a website looking for adventure seekers, people who wanted to live the cowboy life. The only requirements were they had to be under eighteen and expert riders. We walked the scam back. Over two hundred kids applied."

"Wow," Sadie said. "I guess younger ranch hands aren't too hard to find."

"Especially if you're lying to them. Luke called his program a 'Youth Scholarship,' meaning some fictitious donor would pay the one-thousand-dollar fee to have the kid travel to Montana. He would get one of his honchos to shuttle free labor to his camp for the summer. These kids rode in a filthy van winding their way across the country picking up others along the way.

"He promised them all free food and lodging, which Homeplace already provided to similar seasonal workers over the years. It was a good plan for a con man trying to get free help for what he was charging the ranch for their work. He swore them to secrecy and made them sign statements when they arrived, or else they were stuck out here on their own."

"And what about their pay?" Mom asked.

"That gets worse. He told them part of their 'scholarship' included competing in the Settlers Rodeo, which he would prepare them for. The ranch hands would each pay him $500 of their pay for training and entrance fees. He said he was so sure they would win, that they would take home twice as much. Although Luke hasn't admitted it yet, he likely was going to keep any prize earnings to pay off his own debts," Leah said. "And the Settlers Rodeo costs fifty dollars to enter. Out here, they want to continue the rodeo life, not pay off one cowboy's bad life decisions."

These young ranch hands became Sadie's friends over

the past few days, well, most of them. She felt for them. "Didn't their parents wonder how their kids were doing?"

"I hate to tell you, Sadie, not everyone lives the life you do. The truth is most don't. Kitty came from Oregon, and she has no home to go to. Doug, as I think you already know, was in and out of foster homes his entire life. I won't go into the background of the rest. The one thing that clicked with all of them was the horses. They saw their love of horses as their ticket out of their current lives."

"And Justin?" Sadie asked, anxious for the answer.

"He's an odd one. I mentioned his mom, and he comes from wealth. He didn't need the money, so he's a mystery."

"I suspect he wanted to prove himself." Sadie thought of his comments and how differently he spoke to her when he was alone with her — a conflicted life.

"Well, you're a lot closer to being sixteen than I am, so you have better insight into that than I do. He'll be home and away from Luke, thanks to you and your grandmother. His mom may be more attentive after this experience," Leah finished.

"Folks, I need to go finish my work in town. Sadie and Anna, you will never forget this experience, but don't let this paralyze you. There's plenty of time to think about it in the future. For the time being, take a deep breath, relax, and try to enjoy everything else other than this situation, which is unusual for out here."

"How can I relax? This has all been crazy!" Sadie said.

"You are a military child," Mom said. "You've been through so much that your life has prepared you for who you are today. Who else at your age could have taken on this predator? Who else would have had the sense to go back to collect evidence after what you thought you saw the previous night? Even though I'm not happy about that." She looked at Grandma.

Impervious, Grandma smiled. "And who else would have trusted your grandma as your wingman?"

Sadie said, "I never thought about it that way. I thought of how I failed Sunny by not following up on her."

Dad finally spoke. "Aren't you glad you came? Sunny needed you, and somehow you knew it. You knew to not only come here, but to dig deeper. I'm so proud of you." His voice got tight and low. "Although I would like to get my hands on that criminal who tried to hurt you."

"Thanks, Dad, and I think Montana's police are taking care of that."

Dad said, "Speaking of that, Leah, it's obvious you were here undercover, but the way you spoke about Afghanistan was real. I know."

"Yes, that was true. I got my law enforcement training

in the Army and spent two tours in Afghanistan before I decided to come back to my roots. I'm still in the reserves, so still have that military connection many of us never want to lose." Dad nodded.

Sadie said, "Since everyone's asking questions, I have another one, too. Leah, am I finding problems? Or are they finding me?"

"You ask an investigator that?" Leah asked. "The reality is problems are everywhere. Some of us find problems to solve everywhere. You, Sadie, appear to be astute at finding problems." Sadie couldn't believe a seasoned former military police officer and current detective considered her a problem-solver.

"I'm sorry, I know you're busy; is there anything else you need?" Sadie asked.

"I'll need a brief statement from you and your grandmother, and then you're free to go. I don't want to ruin your last day here."

Leah provided the forms and told them what she needed like she was reading military orders. Grandma and Sadie recreated last night's events on paper for the police records. Sadie read through her words. It was like reading a story about someone else's life.

As she rose to go, Sadie said to Leah, "I hope we can stay in touch."

"Sure we can, I mean, you helped me solve my first

serious case in Montana. I plan to make another trip to Washington, D.C., next year for the annual National Police Week. So hopefully I'll be in your neighborhood before long."

"I have another friend in Maryland, Sergeant Lucero, who is part of the mounted police. He adopted one of my, well not really *my* rescue horses, but an Appaloosa, Spot. You two have a lot in common."

"Thank you, Sadie, and I'm glad you're trying to fix me up. But I'd rather meet this handsome Lucky I heard so much about."

"I understand! This is my first time away from him, and I've been okay with it because my friend is helping take care of him at home."

Mom said, "We'll be on our way, and you know how to get in touch with us. Sadie will talk your ear off about Lucky if you give her the opportunity." She put her arm around Sadie's shoulder and walked her out. Dad and Grandma followed.

Sadie waved goodbye and thought about trying to let it all go, as Leah had suggested, and enjoying her last day at the ranch. She came here to check on a horse's safety, and now Sunny would be safe. Then a disturbing thought came to mind. What would have happened to someone as young and vulnerable as Brady if he had been conned into a scheme like Luke's?

CHAPTER 29

THE FINAL DAY

AFTER LEAH LEFT FOR town, the Navarros departed the office. Sadie had not seen the lodge hall empty since day one. Everyone else was out for their activities of either riding, relaxing, or traveling to an off-site adventure. The rest of the guests didn't know what had happened, and Sadie hoped they never would. She didn't need the attention, and the MacKenneys and the respectable folks who worked at Homeplace didn't need this scar destroying the public's view of the ranch.

They left the lodge, and Dad spoke up looking at his watch. "It's time for lunch. Anyone else starved?"

How could he think about food? Sadie said, "Not me. I'm headed out for fresh air and to go take in the horses."

"I'll go with you," he said. "We have time."

Mom said, "I'll go check on Austin to make sure he's out of bed." She kissed Dad on the cheek and left.

Sadie wished her dad didn't want to follow her, but she understood. She kicked at the small stones on their way to the corral where a few horses grazed from the hay bales in the feeders. Hands in her front pockets, she didn't want to talk.

"Mija," Dad started, using his pet name for her. "What are you thinking?"

She turned to face him. "I'm not sure. I think I'm still in shock. I never imagined all this would happen. I don't know what to do."

"The shock is understandable. This has been a scary ordeal for you. I wish I had known and could have been there to protect you. Do you see why I worry?"

She hadn't thought about that. She asked, "How could you have known? How could anyone have known? Not even Mr. Mac or any of the wranglers knew."

"But you did." Dad pointed to his heart. "Right here."

She looked at her chest, not sure why, and said, "I don't know how I knew something wasn't right. I'm so sorry to put everyone through this."

"Sorry? ... We're so incredibly proud of you! Look at what you did! Sometimes you have a difficult time seeing the amazing things you do."

Sadie viewed the horses again and turned back to her dad. "I think I know who I get that from."

Dad put his arm around her shoulder, and they

strolled closer to the horses. "Where do you think Sunny is today? I don't see her here." Sadie noticed he liked to change the subject at times like she did.

She thought about Sunny and panicked. Where was she?

As if reading her thoughts, Dad's voice of reason spoke: "They probably gave Sunny time off after the episode last night which must have scared her, too. That's what this non-horse guy would do."

"I'll bet you're right. I'll ask. I do want to see her one more time before we go. She's been fantastic, and I didn't even know all she was going through."

"I'm sure the ranch will arrange a last visit for you. Enough air and horses yet? Can your poor old starving dad get some chow?"

He moved away from the corral. "Here comes our gang. Mom must have raised Austin from the dead — look at his hair." Dad rolled his eyes and smiled at her. He was trying to lighten the mood. She figured he did that a lot in the Navy during rough times.

"Sure, let's go eat, if it will make you happy. I can ask about Sunny at the lodge anyway."

"Before we join them, please try to enjoy our last day here. No one knows what happened except Leah, our family, the MacKenneys, and the wranglers. They are all sworn to secrecy until this investigation plays out.

Don't worry. As hard as it is, we need to all move on as if nothing has happened."

Sadie pulled her shoulders back and down. "Dad, thanks for everything. The trip, the support, the fresh air, and the talking. I feel so bad. You were finally unwinding from Afghanistan, and here I led you into more trouble as soon as you were getting back to normal."

He turned to her and said, "Don't worry about me. I'm more worried about you. I think we've all learned a lot on this trip."

They headed to lunch with the rest of the family. It turned out Dad was right about Sunny; they kept her in the top field today with a day off after yesterday. During lunch, Mr. Mac discussed the afternoon's event, team penning.

"You'll get to show off those cowboy and cowgirl skills you've learned all week. This is the most fun event, according to our past guests. Don't chicken out, anyone, because we've already drawn up your teams."

Sadie didn't know what team penning was, but if it was anything like the team roping at the rodeo, she wasn't interested in wrestling a steer to the ground. She practiced that with a human last night.

She whispered to Austin, "I don't want to do this."

Austin asked, "Are you kidding? This will be the most fun of the week. Didn't you hear him? Besides, what else are you going to do? This is *the* event." Sadie shook her head but considered maybe it would take her mind off of things.

Mr. Mac continued, "Team One, you poor things have my son, Blake, as your leader. Good luck! There's a reason he doesn't rodeo," he teased. Mr. Mac announced her name on Blake's team. She'd do her best to be sportsmanlike and do well on his team for the other team members' sakes. She was not only doing something she didn't want to do, but she was doing it on a team she didn't want to be on.

Helping the Good Guys today, Sadie spotted a new wrangler who looked like the wrangler Joe without his signature long mustache. Maybe she was astute; it turned out it was his brother. Morgan MacKenney helped out as a ranch hand rather than working with her mom this afternoon. Mr. Mac must have had to think fast between last night and this morning and called in the cavalry to cover for the seven missing ranch hands. No one else seemed to notice.

Homeplace Ranch held its own version of team penning. Each team of humans on horses had a mission to separate a small cow from a herd and then corral it into the specified pen. The ranch divided the teams into groups of six individuals instead of the normal three for official team penning. The cow chasers in these Homeplace teams normally included one experienced team penner. Guests soon discovered why this was the most fun event of the week.

Each team watched those before them and learned lessons of what worked and where to place their team players to make it happen. Sadie's team consisted of Blake and her five family members. They worked as a team and did a nice job in getting their cow in the pen in a fast time as if they had practiced. They high-fived, and the Navarros were sure they'd be hard to beat in this timed event. Sadie was happy Grandma had such a blast, convinced this was her new calling in life.

Sadie loved cheering on Pamela and her family, Team Two, which may have been the most entertaining of the day. Half of the directions to each other were in Italian, and only half the team spoke Italian. The young girl who wanted the specific pony on day one and her mother joined their team, and Sierra assisted as their experienced team penner. Mr. DiLeonardi looked so happy, and Pamela's intensity was a joy to observe. Despite the language barrier, Team Two pulled ahead.

The Canadian girls offered tough competition. The last group of the Good Guys competition today had done this before in their travels. They hand-signaled and hooted and hollered and knew exactly what to do. Sadie wondered if Grandma wished she had been on their team instead, knowing how competitive she was. Rusty helped them as much as he could, but the laughter had to have slowed him down. The Canadian girls ended up having the toughest of the cows, and a few wrong signals to each other turned into the longest time.

Since the whole Good Guys tribe had become friends during the week, the teams all congratulated each other. Team Two won, and Sadie suspected the story of this day and victory would be told in Italy many times in the future.

The evening ended with the famed talent show. One of the guests from the Bad Guys group recited his version of cowboy poetry about his sturdy steed Fred, the mule. He said how he'd imagined riding a majestic, white steed, but instead was rewarded with the most forgiving and wonderful partner who kept him out of trouble for the week. He was the man Sadie heard on the first day of the trip who never rode but came along on the trip to accompany his wife. His "Ode to Fred" poem would be memorable to both guests and staff.

Carrie, one of the Canadian girls sang a song from the movie *Pitch Perfect* and played it on overturned plastic cups, like the scene shown in the movie. Her lyrical voice resonated in the giant lodge room, and the words "You're Gonna Miss Me When I'm Gone" brought the group together about how they would miss their new friends who experienced togetherness out there away from life's normal distractions.

For the last event of the evening, a family took the stage to sing an inspiring version of "Glory, Glory, Hallelujah." They obviously had performed this before, probably at church. Sadie's friend, Pamela, reached for her hand and held it in the air as she and the crowd sang along for the refrain for the well-known hymn, written originally as a poem of unity. Sadie's heart filled. In this song, at this moment, the room full of people shared something special and unforgettable in this past week together, and she was a part of it. Her truth was marching on.

CHAPTER 30

DEPARTURE

AT THE END OF breakfast on Saturday, Blake stopped by Sadie's table. "I brought Sunny down from the top field this morning in case you wanted to say goodbye to her. She's out in the corral with a few others. Today's a day off for them usually, but I thought this was a special occasion."

"Thank you," Sadie said, "and I'd like to do that." She had wanted to do this but was afraid to ask. She didn't want to make anyone do anything extra.

"If you're ready to go, I'll take you," he said.

She looked at her dad who nodded in the direction of the door. "Go on, but remember we leave for the airport in an hour."

Sadie stood, and Blake pulled out her chair for her, a grown-up thing to do. She liked the manners. Sadie waved goodbye to her family and the others at the table, suddenly feeling like a spectacle. Was it the aftershock of the whole ordeal? It couldn't be any kind of feelings about Blake.

He escorted Sadie to the corral making small talk along the way as if nothing had happened. On the final magnificent, sun-kissed, cloudless day, Sadie welcomed the comfort of the horses lazing in the corral. Sunny lifted her head still chewing hay when they approached. Sadie walked over to her while Blake stood outside the corral leaning on his forearms, one leg bent, and same hip cocked to the side. Soon, his father joined him there in the exact same stance.

Sadie spoke to Sunny stroking her silky mane. "I need to go, girl." She glanced back at Blake and Mr. Mac and didn't care if they saw or heard her talking to the mare like a person. They were horse people; they understood. She scratched underneath Sunny's mane like she had many times from their first meeting in her stall and on her rides. Sunny reacted by stretching her neck to ask for more, like Lucky did.

"You'll be fine. No one's going to hurt you again. I know you like to please, that's obvious. I understand because I'm like you. Sometimes it's not easy. We're challenged." She hugged her neck, and Sunny stood peacefully.

"This is a perfect home here, and one bad person

tried to ruin that for you. He's gone, and these nice people over there," she said, looking in the direction of the MacKenneys, "they're going to take good care of you."

She reached in her pocket looking for horse treats and came up empty remembering she didn't know she was going to see Sunny when she left her cabin this morning. Mr. Mac joined her at Sunny's side and handed her an apple. "Looking for something like this?" His eyes wrinkled from his smile.

"I think that will do, thank you," she answered and proceeded to feed Sunny the apple by holding the whole fruit in her hand and allowing Sunny to take bites. Feminine Sunny gently nibbled, unlike her Lucky, who attacked apples.

"I wanted to catch you before you left and thank you again. Remember from the first ride you told me about 'situational awareness?' I told you I thought that was a great term. Well, it turned out I had a total lack of situational awareness about what happened right here under my nose. I like to think the best about people, and I suppose I became complacent about my summer help.

"There were signs I should have picked up on, like horses coming up lame, odd nicks on their backs, and unexplained ranch hand injuries. Most of those kids cowered from Luke, which wasn't how it had been in past years with others. It all makes sense now, but I didn't see it at the time. Because of you, we cut this problem short before any horses or humans got seriously hurt for the long term."

Perplexed, Sadie said, "I wasn't the only one who helped figure it out."

"Yes, Leah told me how Justin sent an anonymous tip to the sheriff's office that got her investigation going."

Aha, now she knew. Leah probably told Mr. Mac because he owned the place, and he didn't know it was part of the ongoing investigation.

"How did he do that? I thought Luke took all their cell phones when they got here. Justin told me that, but he said that was a work thing. But Leah said the real reason was so they couldn't let the outside world know what was going on."

Mr. Mac said, "Justin worked the old-fashioned way. He put his written words in a hard copy letter and slipped that letter in our outgoing mailbox. We don't monitor outgoing mail or communications. We're not like that and haven't needed to be."

Sadie felt better knowing Justin had been involved in taking Luke down. "I'm glad Justin helped. But what I meant about it all not being me was different. I meant my grandma, Austin, and Leah — they all played a part."

"You're right, but you were the leader. Don't be so

afraid to take credit. You had incredible situational awareness to figure it all out."

She reached over to pet Sunny again, fidgeting more
than anything else.

"I have a question for you. Your grandmother told
me you rescued another horse that's at Freedom Hill."

"Hardball? A goofy name, but you know what they
say about changing a horse's name — bad luck." Where
was this going?

"He's a Tennessee Walker, right? They're smooth for
all kinds of riders."

"Yes, and he's the sweetest guy and rideable. I'm not
sure why no one's adopted him, except he's not a jumper,
and they do a lot of that in Maryland," she rambled.

He paused. "If you'll trust me, I want to adopt him."
His eyes met hers, gleaming.

"Really? Are you kidding? That would be awesome,
and I'm sure Sunny would be happy to see her old buddy
here. They've been through a lot together from the auction to Freedom Hill. He's probably missing her!" She
couldn't contain herself and wrapped her arms around
Mr. MacKenney in a hug. She knew in her heart Mr.
Mac had nothing to do with this horrible Luke situation.
Tears sprung to her eyes, and she reached up to wipe
them away before pulling herself away.

She focused again on Sunny who hadn't moved away from them. "Did you hear that? Hardball is coming to join you! You'll have to show him the ropes and help him blend with the herd. You'll do that; I'm sure."

"It's settled then. I'll start making arrangements. Come on, we'd better move along so you don't miss your flight. Come back again someday to check on how Hardball is fitting in. The ranch stay will be our treat as a thank you for helping save our horses, our staff, potentially our guests, and our reputation. I'd go as far as to say you saved our ranch and what we believe in."

"Thank you, and you don't have to do that."

"I know I don't have to. I want to. And I promise, no problems next time." He winked at her one last time.

"This may be bold of me, but can I bring a friend?"

"Of course, and maybe she can ride Hardball!"

"Thank you! But my friend's a he, not a she. He will be beside himself when I tell him."

Sadie turned and gave Sunny one last hug. She walked with Mr. Mac and joined Blake at the fence. Starting her goodbyes, Blake stopped her.

"Don't be so quick to get rid of me. I'm taking you, Pamela, and your families to the airport this morning."

"Good," she said, surprising herself that she meant it. She realized she'd overreacted during their first meeting.

"One more thing … I have a small present for you."

Sadie detected a blush on him, which she hadn't thought was possible. He pulled something from behind him and presented her a lock of blond horse hairs tied in an unusual knot.

"Your brother said you had a lock of Lucky's hair, so I wanted to give you a reminder of Sunny. I tied a few of her tail hairs in what they call a Celtic knot. It probably sounds corny, but it means eternity. You made a difference for this horse, and I want you to remember that."

That touched her. He wasn't so bad after all. But he still wasn't Justin.

CHAPTER 31

HOME AT LAST

SADIE SLEPT LONG AND hard after her late night arrival back in Maryland. The sun peeked through her curtains, and she jumped out of bed, needing to see Lucky. She dressed in a flash and checked herself in the mirror wearing her cowboy hat. She touched the white knot of Sunny's tail hairs that hung next to Lucky's on the corner of her mirror. Still unsure what prompted Blake to do that, she nonetheless appreciated the gesture. That reminded her to grab Brady's gift.

The horses in their stalls finished up their breakfast, and Sadie remembered she had forgotten to eat. She would be fine; this was more important. She heard a familiar neigh. He must have caught her scent before he saw her. Next, she spotted her horse's black forelock and brown face split by a perfect white blaze, with his eyes focused in her direction.

She wanted to run to him but followed the cardinal barn rule of no running. Sadie unlatched Lucky's stall and threw her arms around his neck. She stayed there for a long time breathing in his presence. He didn't seem to mind. She backed away so she could see all of him.

He looked the same. Not sure why, somehow, she expected he would be different. She talked to him and scratched the special spot under his chin. He bumped her head with his hard nose, exhibiting rude horse behavior. She didn't want to scold him in her first minutes back, so instead walked away to get her tack box to give him a thorough grooming. He cried out to her. Did he think she was leaving again so soon?

The empty barn surprised Sadie. The feed shift had come and gone. She'd hoped someone might be interested in her adventures in Montana, but that didn't appear to be the case. She got back to her current priority and returned to Lucky with her grooming tools. He met her with a look that said, "I'm sorry."

She entered his stall again and said, "It's okay, and I understand. I missed you, too, buddy. And boy do I have some stories to tell you." She rubbed the curry comb in circles, and he reacted well to it turning his head and neck in her direction when she got to his shoulder. She was glad to be back to their routine.

"What do you think about trying more Western riding and maybe the high school rodeo? You would be great at it like you are at everything, and—"

"Sadie!" Brady hollered from outside Lucky's stall door.

Sadie jumped, dropped the comb, and said, "You snuck up on me!"

"Sorry, I didn't mean to. I'm excited you're home! And you're taking my job back," he ended in a hushed voice.

"No, I'm the one who's sorry. It's not your fault you surprised me. I was preoccupied. Let's start over. Good to see you!"

"I was hoping to get here early enough for one last grooming so when you came here today, he'd be spotless. But you beat me to it." His shoulders slumped.

Sadie opened the stall door and said, "Then come on in and help! There's plenty of horse here to clean, as you well know." Brady joined her in the stall. "But first, I have something for you. She untied the pouch from her belt loop and handed it to him.

Brady eyed her in disbelief and carefully opened the pouch and reached inside. He pulled out the distinctive hoof pick and held it up, turning his head to the right and to the left, examining the work of art. "This is for me?"

"Yes! It's handmade by a Native American boy in

Montana. It was crazy because all I did was tell his mother I was looking for a special gift for a friend, and she knew exactly what to choose. I hope you like it."

"Of course I like it! I'm going to bring it with me to the barn all the time, and to shows, and to school to show it off."

Sadie said, "I wanted to tell the lady about the connection between you and hoof picks and how you'd helped that young boy in Ms. Kristy's club gain his confidence by teaching him how to pick hooves. But I thought I'd already talked her ear off. Somehow, she knew this was the right gift for you, and so did I."

He cleared his throat. "Thank you, and I'm sorry. I didn't get you anything."

"You're not supposed to! You didn't go anywhere. Anyhow, let's get to work."

Brady pitched in right away whisking the dust off of Lucky's coat. "I want to hear all about it, every last detail. I have lots of time, and I want to feel like I was there."

"I'll tell you a bit at a time, so I don't bore you to death with stories. But I have something important to tell you, and you're the first person I'm going to tell. Are you ready?"

He nodded fast.

Sadie moved to the next phase of brushing her horse with a hard brush and took a deep breath. "It turned out it was a good thing I went to go check on Sunny. She's fine, and I'll tell you the whole story someday."

Brady said, "Go on…"

"Now I need to go check on all of the other rescue horses. I know Thor couldn't be happier than he is here, and Goliath is safe and happy at Maryland Therapeutic Riding. Chance is doing better than expected at Marlboro Horse Farm with his own little girl to love him and show him. Sunny will be safe, and Hardball will be joining her there soon." She let out a sigh of relief.

Brady looked puzzled.

"We'll talk about this later, but you're coming back with me to Montana to check on Hardball, courtesy of the ranch owner!"

"What? You can't be serious? When? Oh, but you're trying to tell me something more important. So what could be so wrong with all that?"

"I need to find out about the other five rescue horses: Vixen, Buster, Spot, Lucy, and Ricky." She left out that she hoped checking on those horses would be less adventurous than the last visit. She'd been lucky seeing the first three in Maryland and hadn't had to venture to a faraway place like Montana.

"How exciting! What made you decide to do this?"

"I need to do it. I lost focus. It's like my fortune said: I need to serve. These horses need me."

Sadie stopped brushing and moved to meet Lucky's eyes. She studied his white blaze, burning like a light of hope providing her the confirmation she needed. "Yes, I believe I've found my true purpose in life."

ACKNOWLEDGMENTS

EACH BOOK IS A journey, and I've been blessed by the people who have helped me along my way. My husband, Jaime, encourages me and listens to my thoughts and ideas, of which there are many in the process of writing a book. My mom offers tremendous writing advice as well as moral support. My brother, Eddy, cheered on this third book and developed another teacher's guide based on his more than twenty years of teaching experience. He believed in this book and wanted to assist other teachers and homeschoolers by providing a fun and experiential learning experience for young readers.

Thank you to my beta readers and those who gave me input, details, and edits to finalize this story. Lori Harrington of Freedom Hill Horse Rescue, Carly Kade, Jim Greenwald, Robin Hutton, Brian Riddle, and Morgan and Susie Ashman — they all had a part in this book. I would also like to recognize Joyce Gilmour of Editing TLC for her professional copyediting services and overall support.

Horses and people around them create stories whether

at home or on the road. I'm thankful for the colorful horse and human characters I've met in life who have inspired me. Thank you to Homeplace Ranch in Alberta, Canada; the former Circle Bar Ranch in Utica, Montana; and the Red Rock Ride based in Tropic, Utah for providing memorable experiences and sights to share with readers in this fictional story.

I thank all the readers of my first two books for their continued support and taking this ride with the Believing In Horses team. Your book reviews mean so much, so if you have a moment, please leave a sentence on your thoughts of *Believing In Horses Out West* on Amazon, Goodreads, or wherever you choose.

VALERIE ORMOND

Valerie Ormond retired after a 25-year career as a naval intelligence officer and began her second career as a writer.

She founded her own business, Veteran Writing Services, LLC, providing companies and organizations professional writing, editing, and consulting services.

Valerie's novels, *Believing In Horses*, and *Believing In Horses, Too*, won Gold Medals in the Military Writers Society of America book awards and six other first place awards in national competitions including the State of Maryland's Touch of Class Award.

Valerie's nonfiction stories have been published in books, and her articles and poetry have appeared internationally in books, magazines, newspapers, and blogs. The Military Writers Society of America awarded her the 2019 President's Award for her work supporting the nonprofit organization and other writers.

She lives in Maryland with her husband, Jaime Navarro, a retired naval officer, and their three horses, and two dogs.

One of her favorite quotes is Alfred Lord Tennyson's,

"I am a part of all those I have met." Valerie thanks all those she has met for their rich contributions to her stories.

Author contact information:
www.BelievingInHorses.com
www.VeteranWritingServices.com
www.facebook.com/BelievingInHorses
www.ValerieOrmond.com
Twitter.com/BelieveInHorses

Also Available

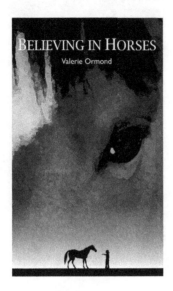

Believing In Horses

First, the move to Maryland, and then, Dad's deployment to Afghanistan. Sadie is in trouble. Then she gets Lucky, a new young horse who proves to be a handful. But that's just the beginning. Together they encounter horse thieves, Maryland storms, and unwanted horses destined for auction and uncertain futures. Sadie makes it her personal mission to save them. Along the way, she meets other people who are dedicated to rescuing horses. She also learns that some people in the horse industry are driven by greed.

BELIEVING IN HORSES, TOO

SADIE NAVARRO WORRIES DAILY about her father serving in Afghanistan. She turns to her love of horses to distract from her problems in her thirteenth year. Sadie commits to showing at the largest local horse shows and volunteering for therapeutic riding programs. She looks forward to her brand new pursuits.

That is, until one of the therapy programs provides unexpected challenges.

And then her inexperienced horse and an unwelcome show ring rival disrupt her first horse show.

Sadie wants to make her father proud. She wants to help others. But where will she find the courage to overcome her fears?

TEACHER'S TACK FOR BELIEVING IN HORSES

TEACHER'S TACK FOR BELIEVING In Horses provides educators lesson plans, discussion activities, and fun learning opportunities for a wide variety of ages and reading levels. Developed by Edward Ormond (AKA "EdUCator"), this 78-page comprehensive guide will make any teacher's or homeschooling instructor's job easier.

Available from Veda Readers at
www.believinginhorses.com/buy-books/

Additional information at
www.believinginhorses.com/discussion_guides

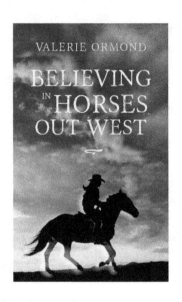

TEACHER'S TACK FOR BELIEVING
IN HORSES OUT WEST
Developed by Edward Ormond
A comprehensive teacher's guide for
Believing In Horses Out West
by Valerie Ormond

Project-based instruction for multiple
intelligences and abilities for classroom,
home school, or individual use

Available from Veda Readers at
www.believinginhorses.com/buy-books/